CEJC
10/20

THE HORSE OF THE RIVER

THE HORSE OF THE RIVER

SARI COOPER

1 2 3 4 5 — 23 22 21 20 19

Harbour Publishing Co. Ltd.
P.O. Box 219, Madeira Park, BC, V0N 2H0
www.harbourpublishing.com

Edited by Brianna Cerkiewicz
Map by Nicola Goshulak
Cover design by Anna Comfort O'Keeffe
Printed and bound in Canada
Printed on 100% recycled paper

Harbour Publishing acknowledges the support of the Canada Council for the Arts, which last year invested $153 million to bring the arts to Canadians throughout the country.

Nous remercions le Conseil des arts du Canada de son soutien. L'an dernier, le Conseil a investi 153 millions de dollars pour mettre de l'art dans la vie des Canadiennes et des Canadiens de tout le pays.

We also gratefully acknowledge financial support from the Government of Canada and from the Province of British Columbia through the BC Arts Council and the Book Publishing Tax Credit.

Canada

Library and Archives Canada Cataloguing in Publication

Title: The horse of the river / Sari Cooper.
Names: Cooper, Sari, author.
Description: "A Camp Canyon Falls adventure."
Identifiers: Canadiana (print) 20190094834 | Canadiana (ebook) 20190094842 | ISBN 9781550178777
(softcover) | ISBN 9781550178784 (HTML)
Classification: LCC PS8605.O67235 H67 2019 | DDC jC813/.6,Äîdc23

To my girls, Alicia and Marley. Without the two of you this story would have had no heart.

CANYON
FALLS
cow paddocks
forested hills

← to rocky flat riverbank
river shallows

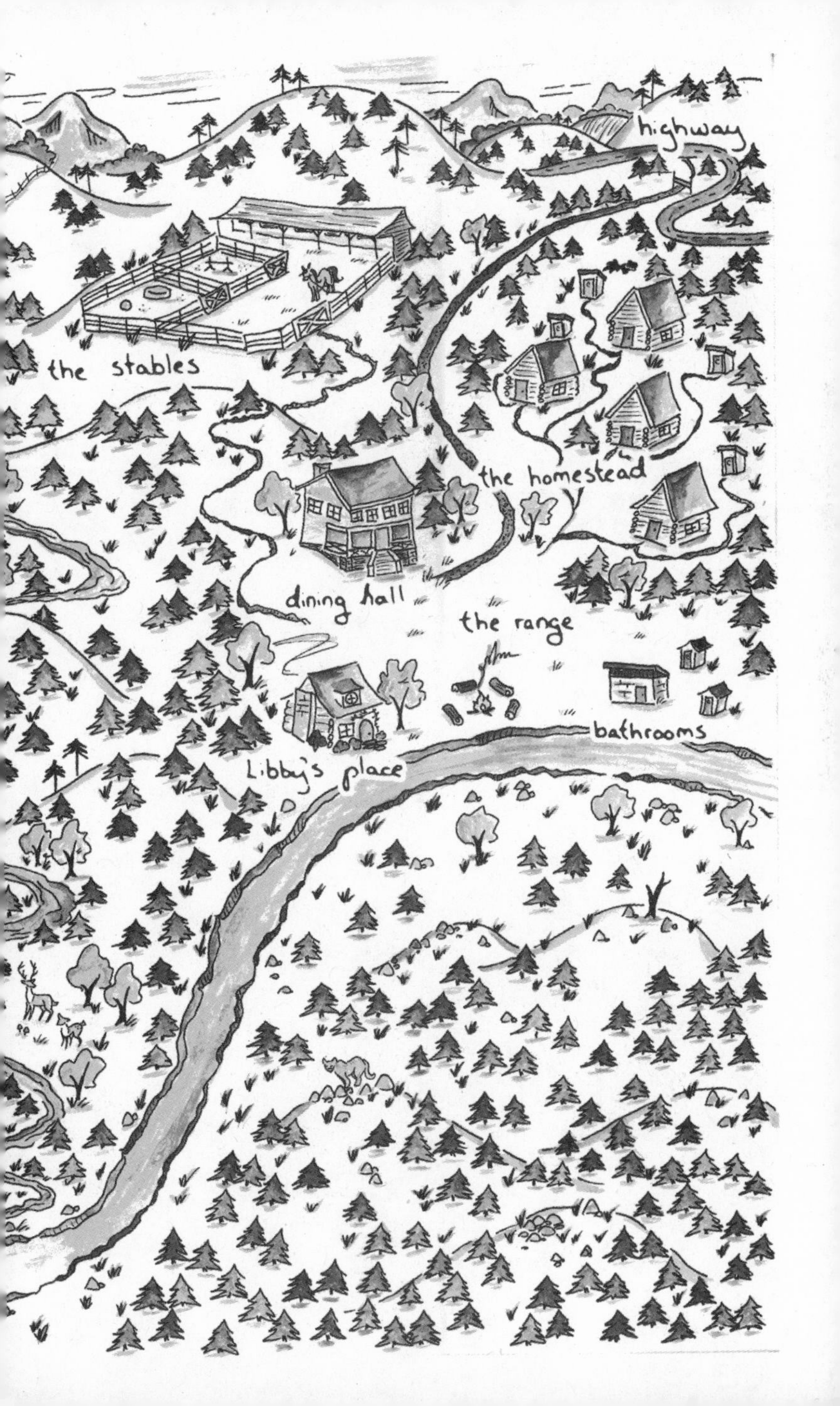
highway
the stables
the homestead
dining hall
the range
bathrooms
Libby's place

CHAPTER 1

GILLIAN STARED OUT the window of her parents' car at the groups of girls gathered around the bus. She didn't know any of them. They were talking and laughing. A tall brown-haired girl got out of a car and ran to a group of three. She was greeted with hugs and squeals. Gillian's heart pounded as she watched. She felt a bit dizzy. She looked around the car for a way to escape. The little voice in her head said, *Why did we think this was a good idea?*

"I don't think I can do this," Gillian said. "Take me back home."

Her parents both watched her from the front seat, her mom concerned and her dad grinning slyly.

Her dad opened his mouth to speak but her mom cut him off.

"Okay," her mom said.

Gillian was caught off guard. “What?”

Her mom said, “You’re probably right. They all look mean. You wouldn’t have any fun.”

Gillian sighed and said, “I know what you’re trying to do.”

Her mom said, “You’ve been excited about this camp for years. The brochure in your nightstand is falling apart. You love horses and riding more than any kid I know.”

Gillian knew she was being stubborn but couldn’t help herself. “What if I’m not ready? You’re the one who signed me up. You didn’t even ask me.”

“I’ve known riding was your thing since we came to watch you in that first horse show at Sunny Acres. Remember? Chico bit, um... Mango...?”

“Rico bit Peach.” Gillian sighed.

“Whatever,” her mom said. “Watching that horse take off running with you was terrifying but you didn’t even flinch. You hung on, regained control and finished the course. You flew over that little jump. No fear! Riding is where your heart is. Go. Commune with the horses and live in the woods. It’s going to be great.”

Gillian looked at her dad, hoping she might get more sympathy from him.

He looked at her mom as if asking for permission.

Her mom sighed and shook her head wearily. "Fine, go ahead," she said.

Gillian's dad turned back to Gillian and said, "I don't really see what the problem is. Your excitement up to this point has been *unbridled*."

Gillian's eyes widened. She groaned. "Oh no."

"*Hoof* you developed a sudden case of nerves?" her dad went on. "You've seemed pretty *stable* up to this point."

Gillian put her hands over her face. "Mom, help."

Her mom shrugged and gave her an apologetic half smile.

"I hope you brought your jacket," her dad continued. "I've heard it can get pretty *colt* up there when it's time to hit the *hay*. Especially when it *reins*."

"Stop! Please! You win. I'm getting out of the car."

Gillian raced to unbuckle her seatbelt and jump out of the back seat before her dad could torture her with another terrible pun.

But he threw in one more. "Glad to hear it. If we went home now you'd be *saddled* with regret."

She threw herself out of the car, but as she did so, she couldn't keep from giggling. As bad as the puns were, she knew he was trying to ease her nerves and she was grateful.

Her mom climbed out of the car, smirking, and walked around to the trunk. Her dad met them there, looking very proud of himself.

"How long have you been working on all those jokes?" Gillian asked him.

Her mom answered for him. "Far too long. He's been trying them all out on me for weeks."

"I have a few more, if you still want to back out," he said.

"Nope," Gillian said quickly, holding her hands up in surrender. "I'm good."

In truth, Gillian really was excited. This was her dream, after all. Four weeks at riding camp with kids who loved horses just like she did. But now that it was here it seemed so... real.

Her dad lifted her duffle bag out of the trunk and started to walk toward the crowd at the bus.

"Dad, wait!" Gillian hissed.

He turned around, looking confused.

"I got it. You guys can... go... if you want," she said.

"Oh." Her dad looked a little hurt as he lowered the bag, but her mom smiled.

"Have the most incredible time. Be safe," her mom said. "And write us! No care packages until we get our first letter."

Gillian smiled. She knew that was an empty threat. But she would write. There was a no cell phone policy for the campers and she knew she would want to stay connected. She nodded to her mom.

Gillian gave each of her parents a tight hug. Then she shouldered her backpack, hoisted the duffle bag and turned to join the other kids by the bus. She now remembered just how heavy her bag was and regretted calling off her dad, but she wasn't about to give in. About halfway across the parking lot, she decided to switch hands. She dropped the duffle and it landed on her foot. "Ow," she said.

The tall brown-haired girl broke off from her group and walked toward Gillian. "Hey, you okay? Need some help?"

"Um..." Gillian hesitated, not wanting to look weak.

"It'll be easier if we each grab one end. I'm Jordan," said the tall girl. She grabbed an end of Gillian's bag. Gillian picked up the other end and the two girls stashed the duffle in the bus's luggage compartment.

"Thanks. I'm Gillian."

"First year? Fresh graduate from Sunny Acres?" Jordan asked.

"Yeah," said Gillian, trying to look more excited and less scared.

"Don't worry," Jordan reassured her, catching her nervous tone. "You're going to love it. Canyon Falls is awesome. This is my fifth year. One more until I'm a counsellor-in-training. C'mon. Let's get seats."

Gillian turned to look back at her parents, who were watching her with huge grins, both of them giving her double thumbs-up signs. She rolled her eyes but smiled and waved at them. She wished her parents would treat her more like a grown-up. She was twelve—almost a teenager. But the little voice piped up again with, *You're really going to miss them*, and her chest ached a bit knowing that the voice was right.

She turned and followed Jordan onto the bus. Jordan insisted Gillian take the window seat, saying she needed the aisle for legroom. So Gillian watched through the window as her parents drove away. A lot of the other parents seemed to be waiting until the bus left. But Gillian knew it was a miracle her parents had even been able to bring her to the bus today. Her mom was a busy family physician and she was always in a rush. Her dad was due at the hospital for his shift in the emergency department. Her sister, Alexis, hadn't even been able to come because, as always, she was at the pool.

Gillian's earliest memories were of sitting in the hot viewing gallery playing with her little plastic horses while Alexis was at swim practice. She remembered running the figurines across the benches while imagining she was on the back of a beautiful grey mare galloping across golden fields. Then, when she was old enough, Gillian's parents had signed her up for the swim team too. She remembered her last practice a few days before, how it felt moving smoothly and efficiently with powerful strokes, and the coolness of the water as it seemed to rush past her. To be honest, she liked it. She might have even loved it at one point. And she was good. Her technique was solid and she was fit and strong and fast. But every club had swimmers like her. Alexis was different. She almost became part of the water. Swimming butterfly, Alexis skimmed across the surface like a rock that had been skipped. She barely made a splash. In freestyle, her arms moved in graceful slow-motion arcs, eating up metres of the lane with each stroke. At age sixteen, Alexis now had more medals than she could display. The walls of her room were decorated with the awards she'd won at provincials and nationals. The other "less important" medals filled two shopping bags in the corner of her closet.

Gillian did not share Alexis's success. At age ten, Gillian had qualified for British Columbia provincials. She finished in the bottom third of the pack. Considering that the meet was for the fastest kids in the province in each age group, she hadn't done too badly. But Alexis always won medals at events like this. Alexis connected with the water in a way Gillian could never understand. By age twelve, Gillian had made the cut for provincials by the skin of her teeth, but she had also made a decision. She remembered how shaky she had felt when she told her mom she didn't want to go to provincials only to finish in ninety-fourth place. She wasn't her sister. She was never going to make nationals or win championship medals. She was sure her mom would be shocked and angry, or worse, disappointed. But instead her mom had shocked her by handing her the acceptance letter from Canyon Falls.

"Don't you have any music?" Jordan's words brought Gillian back to the present. "You can wear one of my earbuds if you want." Gillian took the earbud and placed it in her ear, grateful for this friendly older girl and for the distraction of music. Jordan turned up the volume and lost herself in a game on her phone that looked like the circles were trying to kill the squares as the bus crawled through Vancouver traffic toward the highway.

The three-hour bus ride would eventually bring them to a beautiful valley on a river near Lytton, BC. But on the highway after passing about a million rocks and twice as many trees, it felt like they'd been driving forever. Gillian twisted her hair around her finger as she stared out the window. She tugged at knots in her ringlets as she found them. She glanced over at Jordan and envied the straight brown cascade that fell smoothly over the older girl's shoulders. It wasn't that Gillian didn't like her own looks. She had mid-length light-brown curls, a few freckles and green eyes. She was comfortable with the way they came together when she bothered to give it any thought. But the curls were a nightmare. Her hair was dry and brittle from all the chlorine. Trying to get a brush through it was like jabbing hot pokers into her scalp. She yanked at another knot and shifted in her seat for the hundredth time. Her left butt cheek went numb. She bounced to wake it up and accidentally yanked the earbud from Jordan's ear.

"Sorry." Gillian half grinned.

Jordan looked at her, frowning. "What's with you, Fidget? Have to pee?"

"No," said Gillian, laughing. "My butt's asleep. And maybe I'm a little nervous. But the excited kind. You know..." Gillian knew she was rambling.

Jordan just laughed. "Okay... Well, don't worry about it. I'll keep an eye out for you."

Gillian, a little embarrassed, smiled at her and said, "Okay. Thanks."

Now she thinks we're a little kid. Great first impression, the inner voice said. The voice had been around as long as Gillian could remember. But if she thought about it, it wasn't so much a voice. It was more like a thought that would pop up in her head that she didn't want to think. Her mom called them doubting thoughts. She said everyone had them because sometimes people were unsure of themselves. Gillian had a lot of these thoughts and didn't like them, so she chose to imagine that they came from an independent voice in her head. She had even gone so far as to give the voice a name to help her keep the doubting thoughts separate from the ones she *wanted* to think. She called it Stella. Gillian had tried talking to Stella out loud a few times but Alexis had overheard and teased her non-stop. She was annoyed by the teasing but started to worry that maybe she was going crazy. Her mom told her that Alexis was just jealous of Gillian's vivid imagination. Over the years, Gillian had grown used to Stella. She was just always there.

At the moment, Gillian was feeling nervous enough already, so Stella's negativity was extra annoying. Sure, she had always dreamed about going to Canyon Falls. It was the sister camp to Sunny Acres, the day camp she'd loved, and it ran a similar program. But she hadn't ever expected to go. It was always just a fantasy. She wasn't sure she was ready. Alexis, on the other hand, was quite sure Gillian wasn't ready. "She won't survive a day out in the wilderness," Alexis had managed between giggles. "She's afraid of the dark. She won't even stay home alone for an hour!"

Her mother had defended her younger child. "They sleep in cabins with other kids. They have counsellors to look after them. She'll be fine." But her mother's words were barely comforting. The truth was, Gillian didn't know if she would survive. Aside from the occasional sleepover at a friend's house, camp would be her first time away from home. What had her mom been thinking? A whole month sleeping in a cabin with strangers? Without her family? What if she got really homesick and started crying? What would the other kids in the cabin think? She forced herself to think about brushing out her horse's mane, resting her head against his warm neck and breathing in the horsey smell. With this, her breathing slowed and she settled deeper into her seat. Four weeks at riding camp as far away from a pool as possible was pretty much the best thing she could imagine. If only she wasn't so scared.

CHAPTER 2

GILLIAN STARTED BOUNCING again as the bus finally pulled off the twisting highway onto a gravel drive. They had been descending for the last half hour. By now, she really did have to pee and she was feeling a little bus sick. They passed under the camp sign. She was finally here. She'd read about it so often and now she was about to see it first-hand. As the bus came to a stop near a large grassy clearing, the girls gathered their things and filed out the door, stretching their legs and squinting in the sun. After the air-conditioned bus, Gillian welcomed the warm afternoon rays on her face as she checked out the scenery.

She was standing at the bottom of a massive hill on an open, grassy field that was surrounded by trees. Across the field, she could see a river with steep rocky banks. There were more hills on the other side of the river. A wooden sign nearby told her the field was called "The Range." Another sign pointed at a trail through the trees that led to "The Homestead," and a third sign with pictures of horses on it pointed to a path on the opposite side of the field.

Nestled against the nearby hillside sat a big stone building labelled "Dining Hall." The full-length porch with a three-seat swing and several Muskoka chairs looked like a cozy place to hang out. By the riverbank, there were some small huts and a shed. A little farther downstream, a homey log cabin was painted dark red, and the door was marked as "Libby's Place."

Gillian's gaze came to rest on an older woman who stood watching the girls. The woman wore jeans and a red plaid flannel shirt. Her grey-blonde hair was swept back in a tidy braid. Her skin was wrinkled around her eyes, either from smiling a lot or spending hours squinting in the sun. Gillian knew instantly this was Libby Brown, owner and head instructor at Canyon Falls. She had been a member of the Canadian National Team and had competed in dressage and show jumping. She had even gone to the Olympics before she changed the direction of her career.

"Welcome, everyone." Libby's voice was strong and clear, and the excited chatter of the girls fizzled out. "Welcome to Canyon Falls. Counsellors and counsellors-in-training, please join me." Eight of the older girls lined up in pairs on either side of Libby, one of each pair holding a numbered sign. "Your counsellors and CITs are all experienced riders. Most of them have attended camp for several years so they know how things work. This is Carmen." Libby pointed to a tall, sturdy girl with black curls contained by a red bandana. Carmen held the sign with the number one. Libby went on, "She's the head counsellor. If I'm not around, she's the boss." Libby turned away from the campers and raised her eyebrows at Carmen with a grin. "They're all yours. Good luck."

Carmen stepped forward and smiled. "Hello, ladies." Her voice rang out higher and louder than Libby's. Gillian was drawn in by the enthusiastic tone. "I look forward to getting to know you all over the next four weeks. The first rule of camp is no cell phones." The campers were expecting this but groaned anyway as a few of the counsellors began collecting and labelling phones. The phones would be returned at the end of the month. "You're here to ride, but also to disconnect. If you have free time, talk to each other. Play cards. Write actual letters home on paper. We'll send them to your families by mail."

One older girl called out, "Mail? What's that? I think you forgot the *E*."

Carmen rolled her eyes but went on, ignoring the interruption. "The little huts behind you on the riverbank are the bathrooms and shower house. Your cabins are up the path to the Homestead. Each cabin has an outhouse nearby so you don't need to trek all the way out here when you have to pee at night..." A few of the girls groaned and some held their noses. Three of them started a chorus together, singing, "On the Homestead we pee in the woods, 'cause the outhouses don't smell so good..." Gillian giggled along with some of the other girls but her laughter faltered as Stella grumbled at the thought of smelly outhouses.

Carmen spoke over them. "You can teach that to your cabin mates soon. For now let's get sorted out. Counsellors, don't forget to hand out the whistle bracelets and assign bathroom buddies. I would hate to have anyone come across a bear in the middle of the night on their own with no whistle."

Bears! Stella yelped. *We're not leaving the cabin at night ever! I don't care if our bladder explodes!* Gillian started to grin at the thought of exploding, but she still felt a bit sick at the possibility of encountering a bear, even with a friend and a whistle. Were bears afraid of whistles?

Not likely! Stella answered the silent question. *Blowing a whistle is probably just going to let somebody know where to come find what's left of you after the bear is gone!* Gillian shuddered.

At the end of the gathering on the Range, the girls were sorted into their cabin groups. There were six girls per cabin with a mix of ages and camp experience in each so that the older, more experienced campers could help out the newer girls. Robin was Gillian's counsellor and Naomi was the CIT assigned to her cabin. Robin was tanned with long muscled limbs. Her dark hair was pulled back into a smooth ponytail. She was calm and welcoming. Naomi was shorter with a round, freckled face. Her eyes gleamed and her red tangled curls bounced when she moved, mirroring her energy. Robin explained that Naomi would function just like a full counsellor throughout the session and the campers could go to either one of them with a question or a problem. The girls giggled through the explanation as Naomi did clumsy but enthusiastic cheerleading moves behind Robin while she spoke. The cheerleading continued as the counsellors herded them along the path to the Homestead. But there was less laughter as the girls half dragged and half carried their heavy luggage to the cabin. Eventually Naomi made her way to the back of the group and grabbed backpacks from the girls trailing behind. She pretended to stagger under the weight of two small backpacks, groaning. The girls at the back giggled again through their breathless exertion. Jordan caught up to Gillian. "Hey, Fidget! Cool that we're in the same cabin. You want the top or the bottom?"

"Um..." Gillian hesitated. "I don't know. I've never slept on a top bunk before."

"Oh, it's great! Gives you a whole new perspective. You should try it. I'll sleep below you and if you don't like it we can switch," Jordan said. "But you have to promise not to squirm around like you did on the bus. You don't want to wake up on the floor with a headache and everyone staring at you. Happened to me last year. Somehow I flopped right over the rail. Minor concussion according to the nurse at the clinic.

Couldn't ride for a few days but I didn't have to go home or anything."

Bottom! Say bottom! Stella whispered.

"Top is good," said Gillian as she yanked her duffle bag over a tree root. She wished she could listen to Stella. She was nervous about sleeping on the top, but Jordan was being really nice and Gillian didn't want to disappoint her.

After a short walk the girls found themselves in front of cabin three. They dragged their things up the six steps and shuffled inside. The cabin smelled of pine and the air was cool, just like the shaded forest. Four bunk beds lined the side and back walls in a horseshoe shape. The counsellors were already set up on one of them along the back. Gillian looked around the space. She didn't know these people. The mattresses were thin and flimsy. The floor creaked. It wasn't like she expected it to be fancy, but she hadn't been expecting it to look quite so bare. She chewed on the inside of her cheek and fiddled with her backpack strap. What was she doing here? Her gaze flicked around the cabin and locked with another girl's. The other girl's eyes were wide and frantic. She looked like she wanted to bolt. Gillian thought that seemed like a good plan. She turned to face the door. But Jordan grabbed the backpack off Gillian's shoulder, spinning her to face a bunk on one of the side walls. She tossed Gillian's pack onto the top mattress. "C'mon, Fidget. Time to unpack." Jordan was already pulling her own sheets out of her duffle bag and arranging them.

Gillian buried herself in the task to distract herself from the desire to make a run for it. Not that she had anywhere to go. So she stood on the edge of the bunk below, struggling to make her bed. Eventually, she wound up sitting on top of the fitted sheet she was trying to straighten onto the mattress. But it turned out okay in the end. She had her sleeping bag on top of the sheet and her fuzzy stuffed pony was shoved way down to the bottom of the sleeping bag. She'd been sleeping with Elfkin ever since she was two and refused to leave her behind, even though Alexis said everyone would laugh at her. But then the other girls brought their own sleep buddies out of their bags. So Elfkin was welcomed out onto the pillow where she was used to resting. *Shows how much Alexis knows*, thought Gillian. With the beds all made up, the cabin felt a little bit warmer. Gillian thought that maybe things would be okay.

Robin called out, "Cabin meeting!" and had them all sit on the floor. Gillian sat cross-legged next to Jordan. A girl named Emiko flopped down on Gillian's other side and instantly started talking. Her shoulder-length straight black hair bounced but stayed neat as she tossed her head, retelling the story of Jordan falling out of bed last year. Gillian listened and laughed at the funny parts while wondering if this bubbly and friendly girl was ever going to take a breath.

Robin raised her hand, signalling for quiet. "Okay, how many of you have been here before?" she asked, keeping her own hand in the air. Naomi, Jordan, Emiko and a mature-looking, short-haired girl with light hazel eyes named Mira raised their hands. "And who went to Sunny Acres before coming here?" Gillian and the other frightened girl, a small twelve-year-old named Jaida, lifted their hands. Jaida sat next to Robin with a fluffy white bunny on her lap. Jaida must have gone to Sunny Acres during a different session because Gillian didn't recognize her.

The only one left was Katrina. She was fourteen and from Montreal. She had a slight build and blonde hair in a perfect straight braid to the middle of her back. "I compete in show jumping back home. My mom used to ride with Libby," she said.

Robin nodded as Katrina explained her connection to the camp. "Good," Robin said. "So everyone has at least some riding experience. Those of you who have been here or went to Sunny Acres know something about the style of riding Libby teaches. Katrina, it won't take long for you to catch up."

Katrina snorted a little and rolled her eyes. "I won the regional sixteen-and-under hunter and show jumping classes this spring. I think I'll be able to 'keep up.'"

Stella groaned. *Oh, not one of those. There's always one of those!*

Robin raised her eyebrows at Katrina and grinned. "Well, we don't do a lot of competing here. It's more about learning new ways of communicating with the horses while we ride. But I'm sure we're all excited to see everyone's skills."

A loud bell clanged, cutting through the quiet.

Naomi stood up and pumped her fist in the air. "Woo! Dinner bell! Yes!" she shouted.

Robin stood up more calmly. "Dinner bell ends the meeting," she said. "Let's go get some food."

CHAPTER 3

THE COUNSELLORS HAD all the girls line up in their cabin groups at the door to the dining hall. Carmen went down the line, tapping each girl on the head and assigning her a colour as she went inside. This mixed the cabin groups among the brightly painted tables. Gillian found the orange table. Jordan sat across from her, but everyone else was from a different cabin. Table assignments would change weekly, allowing all the campers to get to know each other.

After a wonderful dinner of roasted chicken, potatoes and candied carrots, the girls went out to the end of the Range by the riverbank. They sat on logs arranged in a three-quarter circle around the fire pit. The fire was crackling and warm as the evening sky cooled to a burnt orange. The drop in temperature was remarkable when the sun dipped behind the tops of the hills. Gillian was grateful for her fuzzy sweatpants and fleece-lined windbreaker. But she kept the jacket open as the warmth of the fire went deeper than the chill in the air. She sat again between Jordan and Emiko as they chatted about the horses. A few other girls joined the discussion, and everyone seemed to want to be paired with a horse named Beauty. One girl said she was silver and her coat sparkled in the sunlight. Another said her mane and tail were long and flowing and she looked like a princess. The campers who'd been to Canyon Falls before all adored her. But she was best friends in the paddock with a high-strung and difficult paint horse named the General who had a long jagged scar down the side of his nose. Because of his personality and his looks, and because he hung out with Beauty, he was nicknamed the Beast.

"Oh man, I hope I don't wind up riding the Beast," groaned Mira.

"You mean 'General Ugly Face?' I heard he ate a kid one year," said a girl from cabin one.

"Shut up! He did not," laughed Emiko. "Horses are vegetarians."

The conversation among the girls faded to whispers and eventually stopped as Carmen walked to the fire and pulled out a long, thick branch that was flaming at the end. She turned around, torch in hand, to face the campers. "It's tradition on the first night of camp to tell the story of the Horse of the River. Canyon Falls is an old camp with a strong history. There have been horses stabled here for seventy-two years." Gillian already knew this. Her gaze drifted over to the camp's owner. Libby had purchased the property seventeen years ago and had been running the camp ever since. Carmen kept speaking and Gillian's attention was drawn back to the story. The firelight from the torch threw flickering shadows across the head counsellor's face.

"There used to be a boys' camp a few kilometres up the river. They spent their time on different parts of the river canoeing and rafting rather than on horseback. On a warm moonlit night in 1973, a fifteen-year-old boy named Ben snuck out of his cabin. He slipped into a canoe, planning to paddle to Canyon Falls to meet his girlfriend."

A suggestive "*Woooooo*!" came up from the girls.

"Yes," agreed Carmen. "Very romantic. But dangerous. The rocks hidden under the water were difficult to spot during the day. At night, they couldn't be seen at all. Ben's canoe tipped as he approached the girls' camp. He'd put his life jacket on the bottom of the canoe to use as a cushion instead of wearing it, which we all know is a no-no!"

An older girl yelled out, "Yeah, but stealing a canoe and sneaking out to see your girlfriend, that's fine!" Gillian joined in the laughter that rippled through the group.

Carmen continued, unfazed. "As he fell into the water, his head struck a rock and he was dazed. He couldn't get himself to the shore. He had no life jacket and all he could do was struggle to stay afloat. The current pushed him farther and farther downstream. He was able to call out once for help. Then he was sucked under the water."

Emiko squeaked and grabbed Gillian's arm tightly.

Robin spun around. "Emiko, you've heard this story before."

Emiko put a hand on her chest. "I know. It's just so intense!"

Again, giggles rippled through the group as Emiko squished herself closer to Gillian. Gillian, also feeling tense, welcomed the squish.

Carmen waited until it was quiet and then she said, "Ben woke up a little while later on the riverbank and somehow managed to hike his way back to Canyon Falls by morning. He said he had been fighting to get back to the surface, almost completely out of breath, when a sudden thrashing next to him made him go still. There were legs and a long dark face and a mane black as the water in the night. Through his panic Ben recognized Hunter, a stallion from Canyon Falls. Hunter had been his girlfriend's horse that summer. Ben grabbed on to the mane and pulled himself up, gasping for air. The two of them were dragged helplessly farther down the river. Finally, the big horse dragged Ben to a rock near the bank. Ben was able to pull himself up onto the rock but Hunter was swept away, unable to free himself from the rushing water. The horse was fighting and shrieking as he disappeared downstream toward the waterfall. He was never seen again. Hunter had saved Ben's life and given his own."

Gillian let out a breath she didn't realize she'd been holding.

"Poor Hunter!" said Emiko. Jaida had her face hidden in Naomi's shoulder. Katrina rolled her eyes and looked bored. The rest of the girls were huddling closer together as the breeze picked up.

"Some days when the river is high," said Carmen, "unpredictable currents develop. Small eddies and whirlpools appear and disappear with no rhyme or reason. A little wave will appear at the shore when there is no wind or boat to create it. Some people believe that Hunter's spirit haunts this river and is trying to warn people of the dangers within it."

A ghost horse? Nope, nope, nope. Stella was not impressed.

Carmen went on. "The river needs to be treated with caution and respect. Remember you can't see below the surface." She turned away from the girls and tossed her torch back onto the waning campfire. "All right," she said. "Tomorrow's a big day. Now back to your bunks and get a good night's sleep."

Ha! Stella's voice startled Gillian, causing her to jump slightly, jostling Emiko, who was still squished in tight. *If she wanted us to get a good night's sleep, maybe she shouldn't have told us a terrifying ghost story! I hate ghosts!*

Gillian shivered. Emiko stood and stared at her. "You okay? You're kind of vibrating."

Gillian looked up at her new friend, embarrassed. "Yeah, I'm not the biggest fan of ghosts."

Emiko turned her palms up and said, "What? Hunter? He's amazing! He totally saved Ben, and he lives in the river and he's a horse and he warns us about currents and rocks..."

Gillian tried to be comforted by Emiko, who happily waved a dismissive hand and said, "Every camp needs a ghost. Hunter's the best."

Hunter died. He can't have been happy about that. Maybe he's not as friendly as she thinks, said Stella. *This camp is off to a great start. Bears, a horse named Beast and a haunted river of death!*

Gillian tried to brush off Stella's worries. But she trembled with more than the cold on the walk back to cabin three, homesickness no longer her greatest fear.

CHAPTER 4

GILLIAN SQUIRMED HERSELF as far down into her sleeping bag as she could, but she still couldn't block out the clanging sound. There must have been about four hundred bongs of the bell. Finally it stopped. What a relief. She took her hands off her ears and snuggled back onto her pillow for a little more sleep. Then she groaned as Naomi cranked a happy pop song on her phone.

"Up, up, up! Clothes on. Wash up quick. Breakfast in fifteen minutes. Be there or be hungry." Naomi yelled cheerfully over the music, way too excited for this early in the morning. But suddenly Gillian remembered. Horses. Today she would meet the new four-legged friend who would be her partner for the next four weeks. She couldn't be late. She sat up and her sleeping bag sat up with her. She was glad for this because the air in the cabin was freezing. She grabbed the nearest jeans and sweater off the shelf above her head and pulled them on while still zipped in the sleeping bag. Her clothes felt tight. Then she realized she had put them on over her pyjamas. She stripped them off and tried again, getting it right the second time. It hadn't been the best night's sleep. She wasn't used to hearing crickets all night, and the wind whistled as it passed through cracks in the cabin's roof. The bunk beds also creaked whenever someone rolled over. And every time she drifted to sleep, images of a ghost horse galloped through her mind. Twice in the night she heard Jaida sniffling and whimpering. Eventually Naomi climbed into Jaida's bunk and comforted her to sleep. Gillian had been close to tears herself a few times, missing her bed and her room, but she managed to push the thoughts away by imagining the upcoming day with the horses. She'd hugged Elfkin tighter than she ever had and then finally she remembered nothing more until the ear-shattering bell a few moments ago.

Breakfast was hot chocolate and French toast with sausages. There was also cold cereal but Gillian's mouth watered with the smell of the cooked food.

She finished eating as quickly as possible and hurried back to the Homestead with the rest of the girls. They all went through the chores of making up their bunks, putting away clothes, sweeping and cleaning up the garbage. They gathered what they would need for the day, crossed the Range and hiked the short, rocky trail through the woods.

They arrived at the stables to find twenty-four horses tied to various posts and fences in the large paddock. Gillian stopped, shocked at what she was seeing. Every horse was covered in streaks of mud. Along the side of their necks the streaks took the shape of letters. Libby was standing at the gate to the paddock, holding it open and waving the girls inside. At her feet was a large bucket and in her right hand was a paintbrush caked with drying mud. "Welcome, ladies. Today we're going to get to know our horses, and at the same time, learn to brush them properly. Find the horse with your name on it. That's your partner for the next four weeks."

"You've *got* to be kidding." It was Katrina who broke the girls' stunned silence.

Libby turned to her. "Hello, Katrina. Lovely to see you. How's your mom doing?"

Katrina wrinkled her nose. "Better than me right now."

Libby grinned, pulled a curry comb seemingly out of nowhere and placed it in Katrina's hand. "There's nothing more satisfying than brushing a dirty horse clean until her coat shines. And if you're worried about the horses, they love being covered in mud—it helps keep the flies away. And they love being brushed even more. All that attention and rubbing. Let's go, hop to it."

Gillian wandered past several horses with other girls' names on their necks. She smiled as Jaida approached her horse confidently, looking happy for the first time since arriving. She passed Jordan looking miserable beside a brown and white splotchy animal. Then she saw her own name. She blinked a few times to make sure what she was seeing was actually real. Her name was painted in mud across the neck of a grey mare with a long, flowing mane. Through the gaps in the mud, her almost silver coat seemed to sparkle. The nameplate on the harness confirmed it. Gillian had been partnered with Beauty. Her fears about not being able to handle a challenging horse floated away. She wanted nothing more than to rush forward and throw her arms around the horse's neck, but she forced herself to approach slowly from the side, so Beauty could see her coming.

"Hi there," said Gillian. The horse looked at her curiously. "We're going to be spending a lot of time together over the next few weeks, and I'm the luckiest camper here." She picked up a comb and got to work.

After what seemed like ages with the comb, brush and hoof pick, Gillian's arms were aching. She had horse hair and mud flakes all over her clothes, and her fingers were cramped. But she couldn't stop smiling as Beauty's silver coat gleamed in the sun. The horse's name fit her perfectly. She truly was beautiful. The mare nudged Gillian appreciatively as she scratched her above the ears.

"I can't believe we get to be partners," Gillian whispered as she wove a small braid into Beauty's thick forelock. "We're going to have the best summer." For once Stella was silent. There was nothing negative for her to say.

After the horses had been brushed clean, Libby gathered the girls around her. "For those of you less familiar with the natural horsemanship style of riding, we teach it here because we believe it allows for a better understanding between horse and rider."

As Libby went on about the style Gillian was so familiar with, Gillian's mind wandered back to the first time she'd ever ridden a horse. She and her family had driven out to Hideaway Farms for a come-and-try style lesson when she was seven. She watched the instructor tack up a beautiful brown horse. The horse clamped his teeth shut, not wanting to take the bit. It took a lot of coaxing to get him to accept it. Then the instructor helped Gillian into the saddle and handed her a crop. When she asked what it was for she was told it was to tap the horse on the bum if he wasn't doing what he was asked to do. Instantly tears pooled in her eyes. "I don't want to hit him."

"We don't hit them, we just tap lightly to let the horses know what we want them to do," the instructor had said. "If I saw any of my riders hitting their horse with a crop, they'd spend the rest of the day mucking out stalls." Gillian was reassured that the horses at Hideaway Farms were loved and cared for. But the thought of holding a stick that could be used to cause pain made her uncomfortable.

After a lot of research, she and her parents found Sunny Acres Riding School, which practised a natural horsemanship style of training and riding. To direct the horse, the rider would pull gently on the reins of a soft rope bitless bridle called a hackamore, which would apply pressure to points on the horse's nose. On top of this, the stable taught their riders how to train the horses. They would play games from the ground in addition to riding. Gillian and her horse would be learning together. She didn't care that this style of riding wouldn't take her to show jumping circuits or to the Olympics. Unlike her sister with swimming, that wasn't her goal. She just loved being around these big, sensitive animals. And riding made her feel like she could fly. She didn't need it to be anything more.

Gillian was brought back to the present when Libby asked the girls to practise putting on the soft rope bridles. This was much easier than putting on a bridle with a bit as the horse couldn't block it by clenching her teeth. They then began their introduction to ground work. Libby taught them the importance of posture, showing them how to stand up tall and look purposefully at their horses, eyes wide and intense. This would engage the horses and let them know that their human partners wanted something from them. They started with a come-and-go game. Each girl learned how to ask her horse to back up by standing up tall and wiggling her pointer finger from side to side with the horse's lead rope slack in that hand. If the horse didn't move, she would increase the signal by gently wiggling both the hand and the rope. If that didn't work she was to shake the rope harder, and if the horse was still not moving away, she was to lift up both arms and take a few aggressive steps toward her horse while sharply shaking the rope from side to side. This final step worked with even the most stubborn horses at the school, but with Beauty, Gillian only needed to wiggle her finger.

Libby then showed them how to ask the horses to walk forward by gently stroking a hand toward themselves along the lead rope. If a girl's horse did not respond, she had to pull the rope toward herself, encouraging the horse to move forward. If there was still no movement, she was to give a single sharp tug followed by more stroking. With the first soft strokes Gillian made along the rope, Beauty dropped her head, walked forward and nuzzled Gillian's shoulder, making her giggle. Some of the horses required the firmer tugs, and finally Jordan's voice broke the silence, calling, "Libby, what am I supposed to do? He won't budge."

Gillian turned to see Jordan staring fiercely at the Beast, who looked around placidly as if nothing much was happening. His head was large and mostly white, but one of his brown splotches covered his brown right eye like a pirate's patch. His left eye was blue and starting just below it, a long scar stretched down to the corner of his mouth. From what Gillian had heard, he had gouged his face on a fence. But with the eye patch and the scar, he looked like he'd been through combat, so his given name, the General, fit perfectly with his appearance. He stood with his weight on three legs, his fourth resting casually on its toe, making it clear he had no intention of going anywhere any time soon.

Libby went and stood beside Jordan. "Shorten the lead," she instructed.

Jordan pulled up loops of rope until her lead rope, which had been five metres long, was now only about a metre and a half.

"Go through the steps of asking him to back up again."

Jordan did. The Beast had stood up more attentively as soon as Libby had been called over, but held his ground until Jordan waved her arms and stepped toward him. He tossed his head, ears flicking and eyes rolling. And then he slowly stepped back.

"Keep him backing up, Jordan. He's trying to get out of doing what you ask. Back him up all the way to the fence," Libby encouraged. As the Beast realized Jordan wasn't going to let up, he gave one final snort and began moving backwards more quickly. She kept the pressure on, moving him to the fence as Libby had said. When she stopped, dropped her arms and relaxed her posture, the Beast dropped his head low, pricked his ears forward, sighed a few times and began grinding his back teeth. Jordan waited another few moments and stepped away from him, lengthening the lead. This time he moved forward with the first stroke of her hand.

Libby turned to the rest of the girls. "The horses will always want to take the easiest route," she said, looking from one astonished gaze to another. "They don't like walking backwards. It's hard work. If they balk at a simple task and then are made to do something more difficult, the simple task all of a sudden doesn't seem so bad. But they don't process things the way we do. That chewing and sighing is them processing the information. Give them time to do that and they will be much happier to perform the first task when you ask them again."

"A good swat with the crop would have got him moving a lot faster!" Katrina's voice pulled the girls' attention from Libby. A few of them gasped. *I'd like to give* her *a good swat with a crop!* grumbled Stella. Gillian fought off a grin at Stella's words and tried to look horrified instead. It wasn't too hard because she actually *was* horrified. She couldn't imagine wanting to hit a horse, no matter what he did. She also couldn't imagine speaking to Libby that way.

Libby blew out a slow breath, looked down and unbuttoned the cuff of her right sleeve. She slowly rolled the fabric up her arm. She walked past the girls, showing them a long, jagged scar that ran up her whole forearm. Mira looked away. Jaida covered her face. A few of the other girls were more curious, then drew in sharp breaths as Libby passed. She stopped in front of Katrina and held the limb, with its puckered and irregular skin, up close to the girl's face.

"This is what happened the last time that horse felt the crop. Three hours of surgery to put the bones back together and three months of painful healing after that." She spoke quietly but firmly. "I'm teaching you how to work *with* your animals as partners, not to try to bend them to your will. Most of them don't need to be forced. Others simply won't tolerate it. The General is a spirited and strong-willed horse. He's bigger than you and he knows it. He won't work with you if he doesn't trust you. But if he does, he can be the best horse you'll ever ride. Jordan has the experience and the character to pull it off."

Katrina's eyes narrowed as she seemed to take in the unsaid words "and you don't," which Libby might or might not have intended. The teenager's lip curled under Libby's gaze and then she turned on her boot heel, stalking back to her own horse to keep practising. Gillian's face burned red watching the exchange. She knew she wasn't part of the confrontation, but even being near it was intensely uncomfortable. She noticed that Libby watched Katrina for a few moments to make sure the girl wasn't taking out her frustration on her horse. But the pair just calmly got to work. Then Libby walked over to the fence and stood beside Carmen. They spoke in quiet voices, gazing around the group but more frequently at Katrina. Gillian could imagine the words that passed between them. She didn't know how Katrina could just move on after something like that. The whole situation made her uneasy.

I've got a bad feeling about that one, said Stella. Gillian agreed.

CHAPTER 5

THE ENTIRE DINING hall crackled with excitement as the girls looked forward to their first ride that afternoon. They talked and laughed and stuffed themselves full of hot rolls and clam chowder, or vegetable soup for the vegetarians and people who thought clams were gross. At Gillian's table, Jordan sat staring at her soup, looking discouraged.

"Is he really that bad?" Gillian asked.

Jordan flicked her eyes up without moving her head and sighed. "Fidget, if he decides he doesn't want to kill me, I'm going to be arguing with him over who's in charge for the entire summer. I'm not too keen on the power struggle theme."

Mira, who was walking by with a pitcher of juice, leaned over the table. "Yeah, remember Rayna from last year?"

Jordan sighed and nodded.

Mira continued to Gillian, "It took her a week to get him to agree to even walk over a jump, but when he was left on his own in the paddock, he would randomly approach it at full gallop and fly over it. Then he'd look over at her and whinny. It was like he was laughing. Oh, and the time she kicked instead of squeezing? I can't believe she held on through all that bucking. Boy, was she a great rider."

There was a shout from across the room. "Mira, we're dying of thirst!"

Mira grimaced. "Oops, gotta go."

Jordan's head dropped into her hands. "Great. Just what I want—to learn to be a rodeo queen!"

"Well, obviously Libby thinks you can handle him. That's a pretty huge compliment," said Gillian, scooping up the thick, warm soup with half a roll.

Jordan picked up her head and shook it slowly. "Libby has blinders on when it comes to that horse. You know he didn't just break her arm when he threw her. He kicked her in the head once she was on the ground. If she hadn't been wearing a helmet, he might have killed her."

"Wow! He sounds really dangerous. Why does she keep him around, especially as a camp horse?" Gillian asked.

"You should see Libby ride the General," Carmen spoke up from the end of the table. "She barely has to touch the reins. It's like since that incident, they understand each other in a very special way. She'll never touch him with the crop again and he knows it. They trust each other. She knows how great he is once he's connected and she wants to challenge her campers to be the best horsewomen they can be. So she keeps him as a camp horse and pairs him with the girl she thinks can handle him. Gillian, you were right the first time. Jordan, take the compliment. Rise to the challenge. If Libby thinks you're up to it, you most likely are."

After lunch, Gillian usually felt a bit sleepy. Not today. She practically flew back up the trail with the other girls. They were all excited for the afternoon's activities.

The horses were tied to the fence and the saddles and blankets were slung over the top rail. The counsellors helped the girls get their horses saddled and cinched. They showed them how to tie a lead rope with a running slip knot and hook it to the front of the saddle. The other end stayed hooked to the bridle. This way the rope was out of the way but it would always be available in case they ever needed to dismount and walk, or practise more ground games. Finally, it was time to ride.

After being shown how to mount, the girls climbed into their saddles while Libby explained what was going to happen. "You're being split into four groups of six today. Two groups will do a trail ride with the counsellors and the other two groups will be assessed by myself and Carmen. After an hour, the groups will switch. At breakfast tomorrow you'll be assigned to your permanent riding groups based on your current skill level. This will allow the instructors to teach to a similar level during the lessons. Every morning half the camp will be on the trails and the other half will be in the training arenas. Every afternoon, the halves will switch places.

"Please keep in mind that just because these bridles are bitless, that doesn't mean they can't hurt. Horses have extremely sensitive faces and if your commands are too harsh, you'll cause pain and possible injury.

Gentle but firm and consistent movements work best. They will feel and respond to the amount and direction of pressure you put on the reins. You don't need to yank. Pull the rein back toward your hip with one hand," said Libby, demonstrating the movement as she spoke. "Those of you on your horses, try asking them to stop."

Katrina, who was already up on Hazel and holding short reins in both hands, said, "What do you mean 'one hand?' And how do I get her to stop when she's not even moving?"

Libby walked toward her. "Katrina, this style of riding is very different from what you're used to, but it'll help you in your riding competitions too. Just try this. Drop your reins and put your hands on your thighs. Then use one hand to pick them back up. Pull that hand toward your thigh on the same side."

Katrina rolled her eyes and shook her head but she did as she was told. Her pull was a bit harder than it should have been, and Hazel tossed her head and resisted the movement. "She's fighting me," Katrina said and moved her other hand toward the rein.

"Try again. Use your right hand and apply consistent and *gentle* pressure."

Katrina sighed and tried again. Hazel resisted for a fraction of a second, then released her head, turning it halfway toward Katrina's knee.

"Good!" Libby exclaimed. "When your horse is moving and you want to stop, that's exactly what you need to do. They're trained to respond the same on both sides."

"I thought I was trying to get her to stop. Not turn."

"You are. She'll only turn her head. She'll stop immediately. The turn command is slightly different." Again, Libby explained and demonstrated the movement. "It's a big, wide movement, not a pull back toward you, so the horse can tell the difference between turn and stop."

"But you're supposed to keep your arms in and your hands still when you ride. Small movements. You never move your arm that far away from your body," Katrina said, frustrated.

Libby patted her leg reassuringly. "Katrina, I know you can't see it yet, but learning a whole new style of communicating with your horse will help you in your riding when you get back home."

Katrina rolled her eyes again. "When I get back home I'm going to have to relearn my whole technique."

Libby clapped her hands together once. "Okay everyone, once you've figured out the stop command, you need to learn how to move forward. We don't kick our partners. We squeeze gently with our legs. If you want them to go faster, squeeze again. Gentle cues should be enough. These animals don't like to be kicked in the ribs any more than you would."

After they had practised moving forward and stopping for a while, Libby asked two groups to ride to the training arenas. Everyone else, including Gillian, Jordan and Emiko, filed off for their trail ride. They followed the counsellors up a switchback trail. The horses were cautious, placing their feet carefully. The trail was steep and Gillian worried that Beauty would misstep and they would fall down the hillside. The mare was surefooted and steady, but Gillian was still relieved when they reached the top and left the trail. They followed a fenceline and passed through a gate. They came to a smaller paddock where some cows were grazing. One of the counsellors said, "Go ahead and spread out. Practise the moves for *go*, *stop* and *turn*. Just stick to walking for today. There will be a lot of time to get to the other gaits over the next few weeks. If your horse starts to go faster than you like, use the *stop* command and he should slow down."

The girls spread out in different directions. Gillian relaxed into her saddle, enjoying the warmth of the afternoon. She worked on the moves she had learned at Sunny Acres for the last four summers.

After a while they returned to the trail, but before they started back down to camp, Gillian looked around and realized how far she was able to see from up there. The river valley seemed to spread on forever in both directions. A bit farther downstream, parts of the riverbank were much steeper and higher than they were around camp. She could see white water rushing through the canyon and understood the warnings about the river. The view was breathtaking, but as they made their way back down into the valley she thought about poor Hunter caught in that current with no escape. Then the trail ride was over and it was time for the skills assessment with Libby and Carmen.

Two side-by-side arenas were set up identically. Half the girls and their horses entered each arena. There were six features set up around each ring. There was a row of pylons to steer around. A soccer ball on a long rope tied to a fencepost sat in one corner.

The horses were supposed to kick the ball along the fence. There was a small crossbar, set just above the ground. The girls needed to navigate their horses over it. A white sheet hung from a clothesline and the horses had to walk through it. There was a raised wooden platform the horses had to stand on, and a small wading pool full of water that the horses were supposed to step into with all four hooves.

The girls were given thirty minutes to try out the obstacles with their horses, and then they were asked to do the whole circuit in sequence. The obstacles were designed to demonstrate the skills the girls had as riders and their ability to work as partners with their horses. It wasn't about how well each horse completed the tasks, but how the riders responded when the horse had trouble or refused. So when Beauty balked at walking through the sheet, shying around it, Gillian was given extra marks for staying calm and taking Beauty in a wide circle to approach it again slowly from a distance. Beauty never did walk through the sheet. But in the end, Gillian managed to get her to touch the sheet with her nose. She got credit for her patient approach and for giving her horse the time to get used to something that made her nervous.

The rest of the obstacles were no problem for the pair. Gillian found out later that the sheet was a new feature and Beauty had never seen it before.

Jordan struggled a lot with the General. She fought to keep him at a walk over the crossbar. He refused to steer around the pylons in the right direction and he wouldn't get up on the step. But he loved the pool, which he splashed in with his front hoof, and he was a superstar soccer player. He kicked the ball down the full length of the arena and then tried to go cantering after it. Jordan managed to keep him at a walk but had to ask him to come to a full stop several times to keep him from racing after it.

After the girls were all through the course, they unsaddled and rubbed down their new friends and brought them back into the paddock for the night. Libby told them they would be assigned their training groups for the rest of the month after breakfast the next morning.

The temperature dropped again as the sun went down, and the girls wore flannels and sweats to dinner. The evening meal was much calmer than the electrified atmosphere during lunch. The girls told stories and laughed about the day's events. In the first group,

Jaida's horse, Oscar, had given his head a vigorous shake while walking through the sheet so that it came off the clothes pegs. It settled over his head, and he stood there stamping his hoof and whinnying until Jaida pulled it off him. The laughter, along with the lasagna, made Gillian feel warm and full. She was tired after the first day. She couldn't imagine how she might get through another. But then she thought of Beauty and she couldn't stop smiling.

Campfire that evening was shorter than the night before. The repeat campers taught some of the traditional camp songs to the new girls. Some of the songs were a little inappropriate, but all were catchy and fun. They laughed and toasted marshmallows. At nine o'clock, Carmen sent them off to the Homestead. Snuggled deep in her bed, Gillian thought of her family and clutched Elfkin. She tried to push away the homesick feeling. She thought of Beauty again and her sadness lifted. It occurred to her then that Stella hadn't found anything to complain about for the entire afternoon.

CHAPTER 6

KATRINA CAUGHT UP to Gillian on the way to the stables after breakfast.

"Wow, Fidget. You sleep like a rock."

"It's Gillian." Gillian frowned at Katrina. She didn't mind the nickname from Jordan, whom she thought of as kind of a stand-in big sister. But she didn't like the way it sounded coming from Katrina.

"Well, whatever," Katrina went on. "I can't believe you didn't wake up with that baby crying in the cabin again last night."

"Jaida? Again? Give her a break. She's homesick."

Katrina rolled her eyes. "She's your age. You're not bawling your eyes out. She's a baby and she's wrecking it for the rest of us. She should just go home."

Gillian crossed her arms over her chest and walked faster. She didn't respond, since the only thing she could think to say was, *You're the one ruining it for me.*

Say it! Stella piped up for the first time in almost a day. *She totally deserves it.*

Gillian shook her head. She wasn't looking to start a fight. Instead she muttered, "That's really harsh." She walked more quickly to catch up to Jordan and Mira in front of her and did her best to ignore Katrina for the rest of the short hike. Katrina kept up, grumbling about how tired she was and how it was totally Jaida's fault. Jordan eventually turned around and said, "Katrina, enough. You're acting like way more of a baby than Jaida. Get over it. She's in our cabin. It's our job to help her get through this."

"Wow. Okay, I didn't realize I was stepping all over the Jaida fan club. You guys are awesome," said Katrina, her words dripping with sarcasm. She sulked the rest of the way.

When they got to the stables, the horses were in the paddock, this time tied to the fence in groups of six, a number on the fence in front of each group. Libby was at the gate welcoming them. "Good morning, ladies. Hope you enjoyed your breakfast. Your horses are set up in your assigned riding groups. Group one will start with Naomi and me for riding skills. Group two has ground games with Carmen and Robin. Groups three and four will be on the trails this morning with the rest of the counsellors. Groom your horses and saddle up. We start at ten o'clock sharp."

Gillian was thrilled to see Beauty roped in front of the sign for group one. This was the group with the highest skill level.

Well, it's not very hard to look like you know what you're doing with a horse like Beauty, said Stella. Gillian knew Beauty made her look better than she was. She tried to push the guilt out of her head. She was happy to see the General at the same part of the fence and relieved to see Hazel, Katrina's horse, in group two. The biggest surprise was that Oscar, Jaida's horse, was tied up with Beauty and the General. The smallest camper, who was having the hardest time adjusting, was apparently among the best riders there.

Of course, Katrina had a fit. "I knew it! I knew she was going to do this to me," she muttered loudly while tugging at the knots in Hazel's mane and tail. "She hates me. I'm the best rider here, and she puts me in group two. I can jump three-foot oxers and do the hunter course faster than anyone else at my club with no faults but I'm in group two..." She went on until Carmen walked over and put a hand on her shoulder. Katrina quickly shrugged it away. Carmen talked quietly with Katrina and she finally calmed down.

Gillian was curious to know what Carmen had said to Katrina, but she was far more interested in getting ready for her first real lesson with Libby.

The arena had been completely cleared of the obstacles from the day before. The six girls of group one filed in and Libby showed them how to move the horses easily from walk to trot. They practised sitting trot and then posting. They went through all the commands they had learned the day before and they did more work on accurate reining. All of the girls in group one had either been to Sunny Acres or were repeat campers at Canyon Falls. Gillian realized that this was why Katrina wasn't in the group. She barely knew the commands and wouldn't be comfortable with them for the first few days.

After the riding lesson they switched arenas to play ground games. They worked on the back-and-forth game and then tried to get their horses to move sideways. Then they played a game of tag where they would walk to the horses, tap them on the shoulder and then turn and walk away. The goal was to get your horse to follow you. Some did and some didn't. Carmen said this was about the connection you had with your horse. She said by the end of the month, the horses would all be following their riders around like puppies on a leash. Jordan laughed at the thought. When she turned and walked away from the Beast, he had spun in the opposite direction and trotted to the far fence.

At lunch Gillian and Jordan could hear Katrina at the next table, explaining loudly to the other girls how there was actually no difference between groups one and two. There were so many good riders, Libby had had to make two top groups. Also, her horse hated the Beast and couldn't be anywhere near him in a lesson or the two would fight. That's why she'd been put in the other group.

She can't seriously expect anyone to believe that, said Stella.

"In fact," they heard Katrina stage-whisper, "I'm sure that's why Gillian is in the group. Her horse is friends with that crazy Beast. Libby had to put them in the same group to keep him under control."

Jordan and Gillian raised their eyebrows and shook their heads. But Gillian knew that she would have had a much harder time with a more difficult horse. Still, it wasn't nice to hear Katrina give voice to Gillian's own self-doubts.

"Don't worry about her, Fidget," said Jordan. "She's probably just insecure. Needs to make herself feel better, and the only way she can think to do it is by making others feel bad."

"Yeah, maybe," said Gillian, unconvinced.

Jordan spoke again. "Of course, she might also just be a jerk."

True! said Stella.

"True!" said Gillian.

WHILE GILLIAN WAS riding that afternoon and over the next few days, she tried to freeze moments in her head, like photographs that she would be able to take with her when she went home. She had brought a camera and had taken dozens of pictures already, but it wasn't just the scenery that she wanted to remember. It was how it felt to be at one with her horse cresting a hill on a trail, or trotting effortlessly around pylons and over the small jump. She wanted to remember the smells of the horses and the hay in the fields, the sound of Beauty whinnying to greet her every morning, the feel of the soft nose nuzzling her shoulder as she picked out the mare's front hooves, the hot sun warming her skin through the day and the cool air at night making her sleeping bag feel like the coziest place in the world. She'd been dreaming about coming here for so long, and she didn't want it to end. But no matter how hard she tried to hang on to the time, it was flying past her like a stampede of wild horses.

CHAPTER 7

BY THE END of the first week, the campers' skills were improving. They had been working on flat-ground cantering and a few small jumps from trot. Now the jumps were increasing in height and the girls were taking the horses over them at a canter. Gillian enjoyed the smoother feel of the faster gait. She was able to rock with the motion in the saddle. She loved the way Beauty responded to the slightest movement of the reins. And flying over the jumps made Gillian feel happy and free. She guessed this was what swimming butterfly must feel like for Alexis.

Gillian felt an emptiness at the thought of her sister. They had never been apart for this long before. Even though Gillian knew that if she'd been at home they probably would have been fighting over clothes and what show to watch on TV, and she would be seriously annoyed by Alexis flying past her in the pool while they trained, she missed her sister terribly. She had received a letter from Alexis the day before that talked about all the prep she was doing for nationals and which drills she hated most right now, and she'd sent hellos from the other girls on the team. After morning lessons there was a brief gap before lunch, and Gillian used the time to scramble up onto her bunk and pull out the letter-writing supplies her mom had packed for her. She picked a green pen with metallic ink.

Dear Lex,

It's great to hear from you. Tell the Arrows I said hi back. I miss you guys so much but I don't have a ton of time to think about it. The riding here is great. We get much deeper into the technique than we did at Sunny Acres. I can't even tell you how much I love Beauty. I was super lucky because she's the one everyone was hoping to get. But this older girl from my cabin, Jordan (she's like my substitute big sister while I'm here—don't worry though—you get the job back at the end of the summer), anyway, like I was saying, Jordan has this horse named the

General, but his nickname is the Beast. She has some hilarious stories about him from training. Like this one time when she was trying to get him to walk up and down a ramp in the arena. He really didn't want to do it and kept refusing, so when she finally brought him back to it for like the millionth time, he stopped, turned around, backed up to it and pooped all over it! Seriously Lex, I mean it was the biggest poop anyone had ever seen! He's got such an attitude, that horse. I don't know what I'd do if I had to ride him.

Most of the kids in my cabin are really cool. There's this one girl, Jaida. She's twelve, but seems a bit younger. She gets really homesick and one of the other girls, Katrina, gives her a hard time. But the other night for evening activity we did Air Bands. You know, like lip sync and making up a dance. Well, Jaida got right into it! She made up all these hilarious moves for the rest of us and at the end she even did the splits. Our cabin won the competition. She's one of the best riders here, but she's also a dancer at home. She says she can't decide which one she likes best. She's so shy most of the time. It was fun to see her so excited about something. But Katrina sat out. Apparently she's too cool for Air Bands. But really she just missed all the fun. She thinks she's the best rider here. She wants to go to the Olympics. I guess she's kind of like you, but meaner. (Ha! Never thought you'd hear me say that, did you?) I hate that she gives Jaida a hard time. It makes me think of that time when you totally went off on Brian McLeod after he pushed me off the swing in grade 2. (Thanks again for doing that by the way.) I told Katrina to back off and leave Jaida alone and it felt pretty good. You would have been proud of me.

Miss you tons,
Keep training hard!
Love Gilly

Gillian put the letter in the cabin mailbag and went to the dining hall for lunch. Their tables had been rearranged that morning, so Gillian sat with Jaida, Emiko and a mix of girls she didn't know very well. They were from other cabins and other riding groups. Jaida squished herself between Emiko and Gillian and stared at Gillian.

"What? What's happening? Do I have ketchup on my face?" said Gillian.

"What's up, Jaida?" said Emiko, giving her a little hip check. "Kind of took my spot there."

Jaida turned to Emiko and said, "Sorry." Then she turned back to Gillian and said, "It's just that Katrina's pretty upset."

"Katrina's always upset," said Gillian. Then she thought for a moment and added, "I literally have never seen her un-upset."

"Well, she's really angry with Jordan for sticking up for me, and she calls you Jordan's mascot. And apparently Mira ignores her, I'm too young to be here and Emiko talks too much..."

"Hey!" Emiko said. "I talk the exact perfect amount that a person should talk. Is there some rule about how much a person is allowed to talk?" She went on, and she was about to continue further but Jaida cut her off.

"Katrina said that, not me." Jaida turned back to Gillian again. "The point is, she finds our whole cabin annoying. She was talking at lunch yesterday with two of the girls from cabin two. She said she wished she was in their cabin. They were talking about setting up some kind of prank or something."

Gillian heard Stella mutter, *Great. Pranks. Those are always fun.*

"Wait a minute," said Gillian. "Katrina said all this with you right there?"

Jaida shook her head. "I was sitting at the table behind the three of them. She didn't know I was listening."

"Good spy work, Jaida," said Emiko. "I'll talk to Jordan this afternoon and we'll keep an eye out for anything weird or suspicious." She made a v-shape with two fingers and pointed them at her eyes and then around the dining room to indicate she was watching.

Jaida and Gillian burst out laughing. Emiko joined in.

Gillian said, "Emiko's on the case."

Jaida added, still laughing, "I feel perfectly safe now."

When the giggles died down, Gillian said, "Seriously though, Jaida, thanks for the heads up."

"Yeah," said Jaida. "And..." she hesitated.

"What?" asked Gillian.

"It's just that I heard you stick up for me that morning. That was really nice of you, so... thanks."

Gillian blushed. "Oh, well, you didn't deserve it. And she was being a jerk." Then she smiled and said, "And you're welcome."

"This love fest is getting too mushy!" Emiko mocked good-naturedly. She stuck a finger in her open mouth and pretended to throw up. "Can we eat now?"

THE GIRLS WALKED back to their cabins, hot and sweaty after the afternoon riding session. Groups one and two had been randomly split for the trail ride, so Gillian hadn't been with Jordan. But she laughed when Jordan told her how at one point the General had refused to follow the trail. Instead he'd dragged Jordan on a shortcut through grasses so high that she couldn't see over them. When they found the trail again on the other side of the field, it turned out that they had cut off about four hundred metres, so they had to wait while the others caught up. The Beast just stood there swishing his tail and snorting when the others arrived as if to say, *What took you so long*? For the most part he and Jordan were doing much better as a team, but he still had his moments. Gillian and Jordan were still laughing when they heard a shriek from inside their cabin. It was Katrina. She had been followed in by Jaida and Emiko. Then Jaida wailed, "Nooooo! Fluffy!"

Gillian and Jordan sprinted up the steps. Inside, white fluff was scattered all across the beds. There were red paint splotches on the floor of the cabin that led out the side window. A note pinned to the window frame said: "Mmmm. Stuffed animal stew! Thanks for lunch. TD Bear." Gillian's heart pounded and she flew to her bunk, climbing up faster than she ever had. Elfkin wasn't on her pillow or in her sleeping bag. She had slept with Elfkin every night since she was two. She felt a little childish but her hands were shaking and she was fighting back tears.

Mira burst through the door and said, "What's going on with all the yelling?" As she looked around she added, "Whoa! Major crime scene!"

We definitely should have left Elfkin at home. What if we never see her again? said Stella. Gillian tugged at her hair and looked over at Jaida. The smaller girl stood red-faced with her fists clenched, glaring at Katrina, who fidgeted nervously with her fingers.

Jordan ran outside and around to the side of the cabin. The other girls followed close behind. On the wall on the outside of the cabin, the red splotches formed a trail from the window down to the ground. The splotches continued along the path through the woods up to a tree trunk about fifty metres away. When the girls looked up, they saw a bulging garbage bag tied to a rope that had been slung over a high branch, then wrapped around the trunk several times.

After a lot of fuss with the rope they were able to untangle it from the tree and lower the bag. Jordan opened it slowly and peered inside. She reached in and pulled out a pink poodle, covered in dirt.

"Princess!" shouted Katrina. Jordan tossed the dog to Katrina, who caught her at arm's length and tried to swat the dirt off. The rest of the stuffies were just as dirty. Jordan passed them out to their owners. Gillian's heartbeat was finally returning to normal as she shook sand off Elfkin. Then her hand touched something sticky.

Emiko squealed, "Ewwww! What?"

"Ketchup," Mira said flatly, after sniffing her fuzzy panda named Panda.

Everyone turned to glare at Katrina. Gillian spoke. Her tone was soft but pointed. "Pranks suck. This isn't funny. It's mean."

Katrina looked injured. She took a step back. "What? Why are you looking at me? Princess was in there too, dirty as the rest, if you didn't notice!"

Emiko asked, "Is Princess covered with ketchup?"

Katrina stared down at Princess, who was sandy but not sticky.

"Yeah," Jaida said. "If I was planning a prank with my friends from another cabin, I would make sure my stuff was involved so no one would suspect me. But I'd also make sure it didn't get wrecked like everyone else's."

Katrina looked stunned. She shifted her wide-eyed stare from Gillian to Jaida to Mira to Emiko, and it finally landed on Jordan. "You guys seriously think I did this? I can't believe it. I hate this place! It totally sucks! And so do all of you!" She stormed off, clutching Princess.

The long silence on the way back to the cabin was finally broken by Jordan. "You know, she might not have been involved."

Jaida shook her head, hugging Fluffy tight to her chest in spite of the red sauce. "No way. She was talking about pranking us with the girls from cabin two. I'm sure she was in on it."

Mira shrugged and said, "Whatever. She's been acting like a jerk this whole time, so it's her own fault we suspect her. She shouldn't be surprised." Mira held Panda by one foot as she walked, so the stuffy swung by her side upside down. "Well, what are we supposed to do now? Ketchup is delicious but it's gross on stuffies. And it stains. It totally ruined my favourite shirt."

Jordan was grim. "Don't worry about it. Leave them with me. You'll have them back by bedtime, clean as new."

At dinner that night, Gillian noticed that Katrina sat alone at the end of her table. She alternated between glaring at a pair of girls from cabin two and firing nasty glances in Gillian's direction. The girls from cabin two had arrived late for the meal. They avoided eye contact with everyone, including Katrina. After eating a small amount they asked together to be excused because they weren't feeling well. They weren't at campfire that night either. Gillian knew they were involved in the prank, but she wasn't sure why they were acting so strangely. And it seemed weird that they were snubbing Katrina. Gillian wondered if maybe she *had* been too quick to accuse her. She decided to talk to Katrina during evening activity to try to sort things out. But Carmen made them split into their riding groups to make up group cheers. At the end of the night, as everyone was heading back to their cabins, Katrina approached Carmen and asked to speak with her. Gillian's conversation with Katrina would have to wait.

When Gillian got back to cabin three, the stuffies were all back on the beds, clean as promised. Several looked cleaner than when they had arrived at camp. And you had to work pretty hard to find ketchup stains or dirt on any of them.

"Jordan, how—" began Mira.

"Let's just say it pays to make friends with the laundry staff, who were willing to let a certain two girls into the laundry facility after regular laundry hours."

"Why two girls and not three?" asked Emiko.

"Turns out Katrina wasn't involved," said Jordan.

Everyone was silent for a few seconds.

Emiko spoke again. "But Jaida heard them planning."

Jordan shrugged. "When I talked to the two of them and told them I would make Katrina help, they made it clear she had nothing to do with it. They didn't seem to want her around."

"Shocking," Mira said, rolling her eyes.

"How did you get them to agree to do the cleaning?" asked Jaida, holding Fluffy up to her nose and inhaling the clean scent deeply.

"Well, once I threatened to tell Libby, and reminded them of the camp policy of sending kids home who wreck other people's stuff, they were suddenly happy to do it."

Gillian raised an eyebrow. "There's an actual camp policy for that?"

Jordan shrugged. "Who knows. But it sounded legit."

The girls laughed and chatted and eventually got into bed. Gillian heard Katrina creep in without a word to anyone after it was quiet. Sleep didn't come easily for Gillian that night. She was heavy with guilt about having wrongly accused Katrina. She decided she would apologize first thing in the morning.

CHAPTER 8

WHEN THE BELL clanged, Gillian sat up quickly and looked around the cabin. Katrina's bed was already empty. Gillian pulled her clothes on quickly and grabbed her toothbrush. When she walked into the bathroom, Katrina was brushing her teeth. Seeing Gillian, she spat into the sink and spun around to face her. "Coming to tell me off again?" Katrina asked, staring Gillian down.

Gillian stood frozen, forgetting what she had planned to say.

Katrina rolled her eyes, walked dramatically into a toilet stall and slammed the door behind her.

Stella tried to get Gillian to leave. *Just go! This isn't going to go well.*

Gillian dreaded having the conversation but really wanted to make things better. She took a breath and pushed on. "Look, I just wanted to say I was sorry. I was pretty harsh yesterday about the prank. It wasn't fair to blame you."

"Whatever," said Katrina.

"No, seriously. I was upset but I know you weren't in on it. I—"

She was cut off by the sound of the toilet flushing. Katrina yanked open the stall door. "Wow. You really don't get it, do you?" She advanced toward Gillian, who backed up a step. "I'll talk slower to make sure you understand. I was supposed to be in on it. The cabin two girls and I talked about it the day before and planned it all out. It was supposed to be at night while I was in the bathroom. A nighttime raid, banging on windows, scratching sounds, planning to totally freak out all the little babies in cabin three." Katrina's mocking tone matched her words and Gillian's face burned. Katrina kept going. "But those girls turned it into something else. They set it up so Jaida would overhear the planning. That way she would tell you guys I was in on it. Then they pulled a different prank on all of us but mostly it was on me. I get pranked and then I get blamed." Katrina's voice wavered for a moment and then turned to ice as she glared at Gillian.

"The two girls in the whole place that I thought were actually cool turned out to be even worse than you. At least you never pretended to like me."

Gillian stood with her mouth open, with no idea of how to respond.

Leave now! Now, now, now! Stella was practically jumping up and down in Gillian's head.

"Maybe if you didn't... If you tried... I mean—" Gillian started, regretting the words as she heard them coming from her own mouth.

"Are you really that stupid?" Katrina cut her off again. "Stop trying to fix things. Maybe in your perfect little life everything always works out, but not in mine. I never wanted to come here. I ride competitively." She squeezed her eyes shut and balled her hands into fists. "The only person I can stand around here is my horse." She was actually yelling now. "Why am I even talking to you? Just... just leave me alone!" Katrina yanked open the door to the bathroom and slammed it shut behind her. Gillian turned and grabbed the end of the sink, using it to support herself until she stopped shaking.

On her way back to the cabin Gillian couldn't stop replaying the conversation. She wished she had stood up for herself. She wished she had said... something. She didn't know what. Perfect little life... What was that supposed to mean? Maybe Katrina should try living up to a perfect sister all the time. Did Katrina even know she had a sister? Did Katrina have a sister? Suddenly she realized that they really didn't know each other at all. She gazed out over the river. The flowing water calmed her. It didn't care if someone yelled at it. It just flowed. For a moment Gillian wished she could be like the water, flowing wherever the current took her, not caring about anything. Suddenly, a wave appeared in the centre of the river, breaking toward the bank, across the current. There was no breeze, no reason it should have been there.

Hunter! whispered Stella. Gillian felt a sudden chill even though the morning sun was bright and she shuddered. For the rest of the walk back to the cabin she couldn't shake the feeling that something bad was going to happen.

JAIDA MADE GILLIAN hot chocolate at breakfast. Emiko told funny stories and Jordan kept reminding

Gillian that she hadn't done anything wrong and that Katrina was a total jerk. Gillian was finally beginning to relax as they got back to the stable for the trail ride that afternoon. She was disappointed to find out that groups one and two were riding the trail together. She had hoped to get away from drama for a while. But she didn't need to worry, as Katrina placed herself at the back of the line.

Gillian felt the warm sun almost directly overhead as they set off. The more senior counsellors knew the terrain well and they always took a different route. This kept the rides interesting. No matter which way they went, the scenery was breathtaking. They would always eventually come to an open paddock where they could practise some of the skills they had learned that morning. Not jumps of course, but different commands and gaits. But they weren't allowed to go above a slow canter when outside the arena.

On the narrower parts of the trail, Jordan went up near the front so the General wouldn't nip at the other horses. He hated following. Gillian stayed between Jaida and Emiko, trying to keep a shield around herself. Trusting that Beauty knew the trail and would follow the other horses, she closed her eyes and turned her face up to the sun. She breathed deeply, allowing herself to relax into the swaying motion of the ride. After a few moments she opened her eyes and saw they had come to the crest of a hill and were entering a forest. Several of the trees had moss hanging from low branches, almost like curtains. Gillian breathed in the pine scent as they wound their way through the evergreens. They often had to duck under low branches and guide their horses carefully over fallen logs.

After about fifteen minutes, they stopped. Gillian couldn't see the lead horses around the curve and couldn't tell why they weren't moving. It was silent for a few minutes, then Katrina yelled, "Hey! What's up? Why aren't we moving?" Gillian heard the General whinny, and several of the horses shuffled in place uneasily. There was a crashing through the brush and the whole group gasped as no more than ten metres away, they saw the bulky form of a black bear running back the way they had come. Jaida shrieked and then the bear was gone.

Robin came trotting back along the line to reassure the startled riders. "All right everyone, wildlife is part of riding in the wilderness. She won't bother you if you don't bother her. This one took off before I could even blow my whistle. We're a big group and we make a lot of noise. The bear doesn't want any trouble. Just stay away from her cub, if she has one. In the meantime, this one has moved on. Let's keep going."

They did, but Gillian didn't close her eyes again for the rest of the ride.

That thing was huge! Did you see the claws? Stella was freaking out. *We just almost died! Can we go home yet?*

As they were heading back to the stables, they came to a lightly wooded area. The narrow section of dirt trail that ran through it cut deep into the ground like a ditch. There were high, sloped banks on both sides, overgrown with tall grasses. The horses near the middle of the ditch got jammed up a bit, and Gillian could see that up ahead the General was turned sideways across the trail, grazing. Jordan was using all her strength to try to pull his head up out of the grass. He turned to look back at her and then yanked forward, almost pulling the reins out of her hand. Some of the riders had decided to steer their horses around him, and the path between Jordan and Gillian was soon clear.

Jordan looked up at Gillian and said, "Don't worry about it. Go around. I'll get him moving in a few minutes."

Gillian tried to coax Beauty up the bank but she refused to go. At the top edge of the bank was curtain of moss hanging from a tree branch. The ends of the moss almost touched the tips of the high grass. Beauty was agitated, clearly wanting to go up the bank, but not wanting to go near the moss. Gillian remembered the exercises from the first day in the arena. Beauty had been frightened of the sheet on the clothesline and wouldn't go through it. The moss and the grass must have looked like the sheet to her. Gillian kept trying to persuade the mare to go up the bank and through the moss.

The Beast, meanwhile, was chewing happily in the middle of the path. He turned his head and looked in Gillian's direction as she struggled. He chewed slowly, bent his head for another mouthful of grass and then looked up at her again. It was as if he were playing dumb, saying, *Is there something I can do for you? Move? Get out of your way? Sure. I'll move. Just as soon as I've finished my snack.* She could almost hear his voice in her head. They were only about five hundred metres from camp and she was hot and tired. It had never occurred to Gillian that she could truly dislike a horse. But the General was seriously annoying her right now.

"Hey!" called Katrina. "Having trouble, you two?" Gillian realized that the others on the trail had gone around them and only Katrina and Hazel were left. Katrina manoeuvred Hazel up the bank past Beauty and was about to disappear through the moss sheet when she lifted her knotted lead rope in one hand.

Gillian realized what Katrina was going to do and shouted, "Katrina, don't!"

But it was too late. As she urged Hazel into a trot, Katrina said, "Get out of the way, Ugly," and brought the rope down hard on the General's haunches. Beauty saw Hazel easily push through the moss and realized that there was open forest on the other side. As she leaped up the bank to follow, she moved into the place behind the Beast where Hazel had just been. At the same time, the Beast, feeling the sting of Katrina's makeshift crop, whipped his head up, squealed in anger, and kicked out behind him. It all happened so fast that none of the girls had time to react. Beauty took the full force of the kick. She took a few more strides before she whinnied and came to an abrupt halt. It took all Gillian's strength to hang on and not fly over her horse's shoulder. She leaned forward and looked down. She saw blood streaming from a huge gash in Beauty's front leg. She turned in the saddle to ask Jordan what she should do, and she realized that the Beast's anger had done more damage than she thought. His reins were slung over his ears, and Jordan lay on the ground near his feet, not moving.

"Jordan!" Gillian cried. "Somebody help!"

She leaped off Beauty and ran to her friend on the ground. Hoofbeats approached and Katrina and Hazel came cantering back along the path.

"Oh, no! Don't touch her! I know first aid," Katrina yelled. She slid off Hazel and came running over, shocked. She hunched over Jordan and watched her for a moment, one hand in front of Jordan's mouth and one hand on her wrist. "She's breathing fine and her pulse is okay. We can't move her. She could have hurt her neck."

Gillian stared at Katrina, mouth open. Katrina stared back. She mumbled, "I... I didn't think about... I didn't mean..."

"Beauty's hurt, Katrina. I can't ride. Get on Hazel and go for help. I'll stay here."

Katrina, wide-eyed, scrambled away as if Jordan was on fire. Then she jumped up and ran to her horse. She climbed up expertly, looked back once and took off at a gallop.

Gillian sat on the ground beside Jordan, clutching her hand and feeling light-headed.

Jordan groaned and opened her eyes. "Where is she?" she murmured, trying to sit up. "I'm going to... oh, ouch, no, I'm not." She eased herself back down to a lying position.

"Jordan, don't move. You could have a broken neck or something."

"No," she said, "I can feel my legs. Kind of wish I couldn't right now, though." She turned her head from side to side. "My neck doesn't hurt but I can't say the same for my head."

"You're still not supposed to move. You should be on a backboard or something, I think." Gillian wished her dad was there. He would know what to do.

"Yeah, well, I might need one to get out of here. I think my foot is facing the wrong way."

Naomi came cantering up the trail with Emiko and Mira. "Robin's gone ahead to get Libby and a couple of other counsellors. We were close to camp, so they won't be long. Jordan, you okay?"

"Very bad headache and something seriously wrong with my right ankle."

Emiko got down from her horse and walked over to Beauty. She glanced quickly at the cut and patted her to try to keep her calm. Naomi pulled her water bottle out of her saddlebag and knelt by Jordan. "Small sips only!" she ordered. The General, meanwhile, stood over Jordan. Every once in a while he would drop his nose to nuzzle her arm, then lift his head and toss it as if to say, *What the heck are you doing down there? Get back up in the saddle and let's go. I've finished my snack.* Jordan reached up and stroked his nose. "Sorry, buddy. We're not going anywhere right now."

Gillian was stunned at her affection for the horse. "He almost killed you, you know."

"No, that was Katrina's fault. Where'd she go, the little brat?"

"I sent her back to camp with Robin," said Naomi. "She seemed pretty upset. She told us what happened, what she did. I don't think she was actually trying to hurt you, but I didn't think it would help much to have her here."

"Good thinking," grumbled Jordan.

Libby and Carmen arrived moments later on an ATV. Carmen was holding a backboard. After checking both Jordan and Beauty for their injuries, they carefully transferred Jordan to the board and rested it across the back of the vehicle. Libby drove very slowly while Carmen and Gillian walked, each holding one end of the backboard, keeping Jordan steady over the bumps. It took them about fifteen minutes to get back to camp and Jordan gritted her teeth in pain the whole way. Naomi and Emiko trailed behind on foot and leading the horses, including poor Beauty, who was seriously favouring her front leg. When they arrived at camp, an ambulance waited on the grass where the bus had dropped the girls on their first day. Gillian asked Jordan if there was anything she could get for her. Jordan looked up at her, shading her eyes from the sun and said, "Could you just stick around until we know what's happening?" Her voice quivered a bit.

Gillian blinked hard to block a few tears and nodded. She tried to think of something distracting to say. "How does this compare to when you fell out of bed?"

Jordan said, "Well, my head feels about the same, but the ankle is new."

“Are you this accident-prone at home?” Gillian asked, hoping Jordan might find this funny.

Jordan said, “I didn’t even tell you about the time I fell off the deck of the dining hall, or when I got tangled up in the clothesline on the way to the bathroom.”

Both the girls started laughing until Jordan winced and said, “Ow! Don’t make me laugh. It hurts.”

They stopped and Libby talked to the paramedics. Gillian was moved out of the way while they examined Jordan, shining a light in her eyes and taking her pulse and blood pressure.

Naomi and Emiko walked the horses toward the stables. Libby called to them that the vet was on his way to look at the cut, and she would meet them up there once she had taken care of everything else. It was clear to Gillian that Libby was worried about the silver mare, but that her main concern right now was for Jordan. Gillian watched as the paramedics lifted her friend, backboard and all, onto the stretcher and into the back of the ambulance. Carmen ran to the driveway and hopped in the camp van to follow the ambulance to the hospital in Lytton.

When the ambulance and Carmen disappeared up the steep road, Libby turned to Gillian. "Are you okay, love?" she asked.

No! Stella yelped. *That whole trail ride was terrifying! That bear running past us was scary enough! Then Jordan was almost killed, our horse is bleeding... Why would we be okay?*

"I'm pretty worried about Jordan and Beauty," said Gillian, blinking away tears again.

"Jordan is in good hands. It's a small hospital in Lytton but I know the doctors well. She'll be all right. If you want, you can go up to the stables and see how your horse is doing."

"What about Katrina? I don't think she wanted... I mean she came back to help and was..." Gillian stopped talking. She was startled to find that she was actually concerned for the girl who had caused all this trouble.

Libby looked over at the dining hall. Gillian followed her gaze and noticed for the first time that Katrina sat alone on the steps. She had been there the whole time, watching.

"Don't worry about that," said Libby. "Go be with your horse."

Gillian turned toward the stables and began to walk away. Then she stopped and looked back over her shoulder. She watched as Libby strode across the Range toward the dining hall and up the steps to Katrina. Gillian was far enough away that she couldn't hear anything, but she saw Libby sit down beside Katrina and put an arm around her. Katrina looked at the older woman, put her face down into her own hands, and then broke down sobbing. As Libby folded Katrina into her arms, Gillian felt guilty for watching. She turned again and ran up the trail to the stables.

CHAPTER 9

GILLIAN CLIMBED THE steps to Libby's cottage and knocked. The door opened and a groggy-looking Jordan stood behind it. "Hey, Fidget. Come on in. Libby's on the phone with the vet. She's expecting you though."

"Jordan! I didn't know you were back! Are you okay?" Gillian was relieved to see her friend. She took in the crutches and the cast and said, "Are you sure you should be up?"

"Well, I can be upright as long as I don't put any weight on this foot. My head still hurts a little but it's really not bad."

"Wow. How badly is it broken?" Gillian gestured to the ankle, wincing at the thought of crunching bone.

"It's not broken, just dislocated. They put it back in the right place but all the ligaments are torn. That's why the cast. It'll heal but no riding for a while."

Gillian shuddered. "It sounds really painful!" Then she thought of something even more upsetting. "Oh, no, do you have to go home? This is so unfair! I can't believe how much this sucks. Katrina caused all this. *She* should have to leave."

"No." Jordan grinned. "You're not getting rid of me that easily. I spoke to my parents last night and they wanted me to come home but I don't want to leave. I can still get around on the crutches. I can groom some of the counsellors' horses and Libby said I can help with the ground work classes.

"They said that I have a mild concussion, so I slept here last night. They thought I should stay with an adult. Poor Libby was up most of the night waking me up every couple of hours to make sure I hadn't died in my sleep. The doctors said she didn't need to do that but it seemed to make her feel better.

"And as for Katrina, she's grounded for three days. No riding. She'll be mucking out the paddocks. But Libby said she was pretty broken up about what happened. She wasn't trying to hurt me. She just kind of forgot who she was dealing with when she swatted the General. Any other horse probably would have just gotten out of the way."

"But she should have known better. She heard the story about the last time he was hit." Gillian couldn't help sounding whinier than she wanted to.

"Yeah, it was stupid. That's why she's grounded. But I think she shocked herself this time. Look, I'm not really supposed to say anything. I guess Libby was worried about me going off on Katrina, so she told me that Katrina's mom dumped her up here so she could spend time with her new boyfriend. The guy doesn't like kids. And then after the stuffy prank, Katrina lost it and asked to go home. Libby called her mom but she refused to come get her. Said something about the experience toughening her up or something, but I don't think Libby thought that was the real reason she wouldn't come. Anyway, it might explain why Katrina's been such a brat this summer. But from what I heard she was really freaked out about this. I seriously doubt anything like it will happen again."

Gillian thought of her own family. They weren't perfect but at least she knew they loved her. Hearing Katrina's story didn't make her actions okay, but it did make her seem a little more human.

Gillian frowned, confused. "So if *you're* telling me all this, why does Libby want to see me?"

Jordan's face grew grimmer. "Go on into her office and sit down. She'll be there in a minute." Jordan pointed the way for her.

Libby's office was warm and informal. There were a lot of places to sit so Gillian assumed it must be where Libby held the staff meetings. There was a small computer desk in one corner. In a circle around the room were some cushioned chairs and a small sofa, but Gillian, feeling like she'd been sent to the principal's office, chose a hard-backed wooden chair that looked like it once belonged to a dining set.

Yep. Perfect choice, said Stella. Gillian squeezed her eyes shut, trying to make Stella be quiet, but the voice continued anyway. *This is definitely the getting-bad-news chair.*

"Why do you think it's bad news? Maybe she just wants to thank me for helping yesterday," Gillian said out loud. Then feeling silly, she scanned the room to make sure no one was around to hear her.

No way. You're just as nervous as I am, Stella went on. *You saw Beauty's leg. What do you think you're going to be doing for the rest of the summer now that you don't have a horse to ride?*

Gillian reached up and wound a curl around her finger. She gave it a good tug and then winced. The counsellors had made her leave the stables yesterday afternoon to get ready for dinner before the vet had finished examining Beauty and Gillian didn't know how bad the injury was. She'd been at camp for almost two weeks already and she couldn't imagine starting over with a new horse. She'd gotten to know Beauty so well in such a short time. She balled up her fists and willed Stella to shut up, but her eyes stung with the threat of tears.

After a few moments, Libby walked in, followed by Jordan on her crutches. "Hi, Gillian," Libby began. "I wanted to thank you for all your help yesterday. You stepped up in an emergency and helped look after your friend. You were able to stay calm, which is a fantastic quality to have in a crisis."

Gillian looked over at Jordan, who nodded in agreement. "Yeah, thanks, Fidget."

Gillian said, "You're welcome, I guess." She looked back at Libby. "I wasn't really thinking about it. I just wanted Jordan to be okay."

"Well, you're a good friend." Libby smiled and put her hand over Gillian's on the arm of the chair.

Uh oh, Stella said. *Here it comes.*

"Here's the thing," Libby said. "Beauty's leg is going to be fine, once it heals."

"Once it heals..." Gillian repeated, chewing on the inside of her cheek.

"Yes. She can't be ridden until it heals."

Gillian wound a curl tightly around her finger. "So what do I do now? There's no horse for me."

"Actually, one just became available. I can't ride until I heal either," Jordan added.

"What?" gasped Gillian.

Told you! Bad news. Actually, that's even worse news than I expected. Stella sounded surprised that she hadn't thought of the worst-case scenario.

"No way!" Gillian said. "I can't ride him. Jordan, you're amazing and you had trouble. How am I supposed to control him?"

Libby stopped her. "You're not. You're supposed to learn to work with him, to get him to understand what you want."

"Libby, I get that, but we're talking about the Beast."

"Actually, his name is the General. The counsellors

and I all agreed that you can manage this with close supervision and help. Jordan will be there during ground training and she can help you figure out what works and what doesn't. I'll be there during lessons and we'll do extra training for you instead of trail rides over the next few days to get you two caught up."

"Can't one of the counsellors ride him and I can just take her horse?"

"No, they would need to learn how to work with him too, and during that time, they wouldn't be able to act as trail guides. I need all of them on their horses. But trust me. I wouldn't put you on him if I didn't think you could do it. You're an excellent rider for your age. You may not have the experience some of the other girls have, but you connected with Beauty right away."

"But that was her. She made me look good. Everyone wanted to be partnered with her."

Jordan grinned. "Yeah, everyone likes her because she's pretty. But she's not an easy horse. Her best friend is the General, remember? Most years she gives her rider a lot of attitude. But not you. It was actually pretty amazing to see."

Gillian shook her head. She couldn't believe what she was hearing. She was sure she'd been riding so well because she had such an easygoing horse. Beauty was difficult? Gillian took a deep breath and blew it out slowly, still not convinced, but she couldn't really think of any way out of it. "When do we start?"

"Now," said Libby.

"But I have to go back to the cabin and clean my bunk," Gillian said, hoping to put it off at least a little longer.

"Actually, Katrina has volunteered to do that this morning. She feels more than a little responsible for you being in this situation."

Gillian shook her head again. This was too weird. *Check your sleeping bag before you get in tonight*, warned Stella. *There might be a snake in there!*

CHAPTER 10

Dear Lex,

I loved your last letter. Practice sounds brutal but at least you've had time to have a little fun. I can't believe you guys got together to watch *The Mighty Ducks* for team building. You're so weird. But I guess there aren't too many inspirational swimming movies.

To answer mom's question, yes, the weather has been okay. It hasn't rained all summer, but the river's still pretty fast in some parts. We walk by it on our trail rides. It's so hot when the sun is up over the edge of the hills, but it still gets really cold at night. Thanks for lending me those fleece pyjamas. (I figured you probably noticed by now that they were missing. Haha.)

Things have been going okay since I started working with the Beast. Not great, but okay. The annoying girls in cabin two started taking bets on how long I'm going to last and whether I'm going to quit or wind up mangled. I'm going to get through it, though. You'll see. It started out a bit rough three days ago. The first two ground games were fine but when we got to the back-and-forth game, it was less smooth. The Beast backed up fine. But when I tried to bring him forward, he wouldn't come no matter how aggressively I asked him. So I backed him up farther and then went back down to the gentlest stroking command. He walked forward easily that time and I thought we had a breakthrough... Right up until he brought his hoof down on my foot. Then he refused to move a step! Didn't matter how loud I yelled. (I know yelling isn't really part of this style of training but remember when you accidentally slammed my hand in the car door? That's how much this hurt!) Jordan talked me through it. She got me to stop yelling and showed me how to use the porcupine game. Basically, horses have this reflex where if you push them to try to get them to move they lean into the push. In this game called porcupine, you use increasing pressure to teach them to move when you want them to. We were able to get him off my foot that way. It was weird, though. At first when I was pushing him and still yelling, I got a good look at his eyes. He was totally staring me down! It was like he knew what he was doing and he was testing me to see how I would react. Maybe he was checking to see if I would hit him. I don't know. Ever since then, he looks at me differently. We seem to understand each other a little better and he's more willing to follow my commands. And I can still use my foot! (It's a little bruised but nothing too serious.)

Libby's been coaching us in the riding ring and things are getting better. We even did the low jump from trot today. Beauty's leg is healing but she can't be ridden for a few weeks. Katrina's finally done with her grounding. She isn't really talking much to anyone lately. But today when I was on my way into the shower and she was on her way out, she caught my eye and she kind of, almost, maybe smiled at me. A real smile. It was small but there was nothing mean behind it. Then she went back to looking sad and walked off. Also Jaida seems to be over the worst of her homesickness. I asked her about it yesterday and she said that Jordan getting hurt made her realize that there are worse things than being away from home. Jordan's ankle is still in a cast but it hurts less, which is great because her help with the Beast is what's really getting me through.

Keep practising hard. Write me as soon as you get back from training camp in Victoria. I want to hear all about it. How cool that you'll be swimming in the same pool as some of the Olympic team. Talk about motivation!

Miss you tons,

Gilly

CHAPTER 11

"LADIES! LISTEN UP!" Carmen had to shout to be heard over the lunchtime clatter. She waited and then eventually blew a short, sharp blast on her bear whistle. The noise stopped instantly and she spoke. "Today is supposed to be the last day of the heat wave." Gillian cheered along with the rest of the girls. She was currently holding her cup of cold water against her chest trying to cool off. It had been over thirty degrees for the last five days. On the trails they could stay in the trees, but the heat was almost unbearable in the arenas.

"But this afternoon is going to be the hottest that it's been before the cold front moves in this evening!" Carmen added. Groans echoed throughout the dining hall. "So there will be special programming for the afternoon. Arena training for groups three and four will all be ground games today. It's too hot for the horses to wear saddles and blankets in the full sun. We'll have extra wading pools set up for the horses to keep cool, but your classes might be cut short." There were a few *awws* of disappointment followed by someone shouting, "Can *we* get in the wading pools to keep cool?" Then the *awws* changed to *ewws*.

Carmen waited until it was quiet again. "The trail groups should still be okay to ride but we might have to get creative. Clear your tables, head back to your cabins, put on tons of sunscreen, fill your water bottles and meet at the stables. Oh, and maybe wear swimsuits under your riding gear. No, you will *not* be getting in the wading pools. But you will have a chance to cool off." To Gillian, that sounded amazing. An excited murmur buzzed through the dining hall while the girls cleaned off their tables.

When they arrived at the paddocks, groups three and four led their untacked horses to the arenas for ground training. The trail groups tacked up and climbed into their saddles. Naomi and the counsellors from cabin four were leading the trail ride today, and they gathered the girls into a group. Naomi said, "Before we head out today, you need to know there'll be some difficult terrain. We're going a bit farther than usual but it'll be worth it. Gillian, you'll ride second with one of us in front and one behind. Since it's your first trail ride with the General, we'll help you out if you run into... challenges." Gillian squirmed in her saddle at the word *challenges*, even though she was going to be sandwiched between two counsellors.

Pretend we're sick! Our stomach hurts! We have malaria! We can't do this! Stella's plan was tempting but Gillian gritted her teeth. She saw the cabin two girls eyeing her and she thought of them betting on when she would quit. She pictured Alexis, her perfect sister with all her medals, and herself with one more failure. She couldn't back down, no matter how scared she was. Stella always got to her. Gillian wasn't going to let her this time.

Gillian fired back at Stella. *We'll be fine!*

Whatever, Stella muttered. *You're the boss. But if we die, I'm going to be seriously annoyed.*

The trail started with a steep climb up the hillside. They travelled downstream on a winding path through the forest. After a while, the ground was rockier. Through a break in the trees Gillian could see they were now high above the river. Then the counsellors led them to a path that wound back down toward the riverbank. The girls had to lean way back in their saddles while the horses picked their way down the hill. Jaida and Oscar were somewhere in the middle of the pack. Katrina and Hazel were at the back with only the third counsellor behind them. The General, up near the front, chose his footsteps carefully. He seemed to enjoy the difficult terrain and while he was navigating it, Gillian gave him some loose rein. But she still gripped it tightly with one hand in case she needed to take control.

Even in the shaded areas the girls were red-faced and the horses were sweating. After a final steep descent, Gillian was relieved to reach the end of the trail. She saw that they stood in a rocky clearing near the water. The clearing was surrounded by the hills. A stream burbled past them and emptied into the river. The girls dismounted and took the horses to the edge of the stream so they could drink. The Beast took several long swallows and then pawed at the stream with his hoof. He stamped anxiously. When Gillian was sure he didn't want to drink any more, she led him away from the water. She ran her hands over him and talked to him softly to settle him down.

Naomi stood in the middle of the clearing and called for the girls' attention. Gillian looked up, pulling her focus away from her horse.

Naomi gestured to the shoreline behind her. The riverbank stood about a metre above the water level except for one section in the middle. That area was about two metres wide and sloped down to the water like a ramp. Naomi said, "This is one of the only places near camp that we can easily access a section of the river that's calm and shallow close to shore. Anyone up for a dip?"

The girls looked at each other excitedly. A dip in the river was just what they'd hoped for when they'd been told to wear their swimsuits.

"But we don't have towels," said Jaida.

The counsellors all began pulling chamois-style towels out of their saddlebags. They had enough for all the campers. Naomi, a certified lifeguard, would watch the girls in the water while the other counsellors would stay with the horses.

The girls took off their riding gear and clothes. They were told to stay within ten metres of the shore and not to swim past the edge of the clearing downstream because the water got a whole lot deeper and there were hidden rocks and unpredictable currents. Between the edges of the clearing, they would be safe.

Gillian walked in until she was up to her waist. She turned to look downstream, and she could see the banks rising up into cliff walls. This must be the area she had seen from above during their first trail ride. In the sheltered section of the river near the clearing, she couldn't feel a current at all. The water was colder than she expected and the sensation on her skin was completely refreshing. She dove in and swam a few strokes out. Then she turned and swam parallel to the riverbank. Making sure not to go past the safe area downstream, she executed a slow tumble turn before the edge of the clearing and swam back the other way at a slightly faster pace. She kept swimming lengths, using the edges of the clearing as her turning points. After several lengths of front crawl, she spread her arms out into a graceful butterfly stroke, eating up the distance with powerful dolphin kicks. Gasping from effort, she rolled onto her back and stared at the sky. When her breathing settled back to normal, she breast stroked back in until the water was waist-deep. She stood up and looked back at the bank. A few of the girls were splashing and playing near the water's edge, but several were staring at her.

She waded the rest of the way back to the group, surprised at how good it had felt to do the familiar strokes, to stretch out her body and feel it glide through the water. When she got back to the shore, all the splashing had stopped and the whole group was looking at her.

"You're amazing!" Jaida blurted. Gillian shrugged. Jaida stared at her, eyes wide. "No, seriously. You're incredible."

"Yeah," admitted Gillian. "Well, that's my other life."

"Don't you like it? You must win a lot of races."

"Some. But not as many as my sister. She's seeded to win medals at nationals. I've never been as good as her."

"That's rough," said Jaida. The rest of the group had gone back to playing in the cool water.

"Not really," said Gillian, realizing it was true as she said it. "It's cool that she's so good at it."

"And riding is your thing anyway," said Jaida.

"Yeah, I definitely love to ride. But I didn't realize how much I missed swimming until now. Maybe swimming can be one of my things even if my sister will always be faster, even if I never make nationals."

"Yeah!" Jaida smiled widely. "Like me with dance. I love it. It takes time away from my riding so I'll never be a superstar at either one. But that's okay because I get to do two things I love."

Gillian looked at Jaida thoughtfully. "You know what else I love?"

Jaida shook her head.

Gillian used both hands to shove a giant wave right at Jaida's face as she yelled, "Water fight!"

Jaida shrieked with laughter and started chasing Gillian toward the others, who quickly joined in. And suddenly the hills echoed with the sounds of splashing and laughter.

CHAPTER 12

AFTER FIFTEEN MINUTES of epic battle, the waterlogged girls dried off. Gillian and a few of the other girls put their clothes back on over their damp suits to help them stay cool in the scorching afternoon heat. Naomi then explained that they were going to ride the horses into the river. She told the girls to keep close to shore and to stay at a walk. They would only stay in for a few minutes. But it would be a nice opportunity for the horses to cool off. "Oh," she added, "and no jumping in off the edge of the riverbank. It's way too steep. Everyone mount and form a line at the sloped entry area."

The General seemed agitated when Gillian approached him, and she tried to settle him as much as she could. One of the counsellors had Gillian play the back-and-forth game with him a few times near the stream, while the other girls climbed into their saddles. After this, he seemed to relax back into their partnership. By the time Gillian pulled herself into the saddle, the Beast was fairly calm.

They walked toward the entry point and joined the back of the line. One counsellor stayed with Gillian. One was at the entry point helping the horses get safely into the water. Naomi and her horse were already in the river along with several camper and horse pairs. Just like on the obstacle course, some of the horses took to it right away. They splashed and drank and high-stepped around, while others were much more cautious, taking their time getting their feet wet. Gillian smiled as she watched the playful activity, excited to get in with her own horse. The Beast stamped his feet impatiently. He flicked his ears forward and back, and tossed his head. Gillian patted his neck and talked soothingly. He took a step sideways to get around the horse in front of him. She pulled for a stop. He resisted. She tried again and he turned his head. She relaxed, thinking he was listening. But instead he just moved to the other side and was suddenly pushing his way past the line. Gillian tugged too hard and he yanked his head forward, pulling the reins through her hand. He suddenly had full control and he picked up a trot toward the river. Gillian lost the footing in her stirrups. She tried to gather the reins back while bouncing in the saddle. She grabbed a fistful of his mane to keep from falling off. "Hey! Beast, whoa!" she shouted. He tried to push his way through to the front of the line, but the other horses kicked out when he got too close.

"Gillian, what are you doing?" Naomi called to her. "Get him back in line."

"I'm trying!" Gillian called back. At this point she realized she was no more than a passenger. The counsellors were trying to get to her, but the Beast was trotting up and down the line looking for an opening. Finally he reared up slightly, spun and headed to the edge of the raised riverbank. He stopped for a moment, stared down at the river and gathered himself. Gillian finally managed to get her feet back in the stirrups and collect the reins while still gripping tight to the out-of-control horse's mane. She stared over his shoulder at the one-metre drop and yelled, "Beast, no!" as he leaped.

She fought to stay in the saddle and barely managed to keep from flying over his head as they landed with a splash. He bounded farther into the river and stopped for a moment, dipping his head right into the water. Gillian was pulled forward as he did this. She steadied herself, and then he raised his head and shook it, spraying droplets everywhere. He lifted his right front hoof and began pawing at the water, splashing his belly and soaking Gillian.

"You crazy animal!" she shouted. "Cut it out!"

He turned his head to look at her and lurched forward, picking up a high-footed trot downstream. She was signalling *turn, stop,* whatever she could to try to take back control, but he was enjoying himself far too much to pay attention. He trotted another few metres downstream, then wheeled around and trotted back up. Naomi called out instructions and Gillian followed them as if her life depended on it, which at this point, she thought it might, but nothing worked. The Beast turned and splashed his way downstream and away from the bank. The water was now up to his shoulder and the shouts from the counsellors were getting fainter and farther away.

Suddenly Gillian became aware of the current. She gave up trying to control the Beast and simply hung on, hoping he would turn around soon on his own.

She thought about jumping off a few times, but the water was dark and she knew there could be rocks just below the surface. Then the saddle beneath her was gone. She was suspended in mid-air for a second and then she was in the water, fighting to keep her head above the surface. She was being pulled farther downstream. She spun around, looking for the Beast. His head popped up a few metres upstream from her. He was swimming back the way they had come. She realized they must have reached the point where the ground dropped away. He had turned back instantly and she had been thrown forward into the current. She could still see the counsellors waving frantically but she couldn't hear them anymore. Here the river was deep and powerful. Gillian was swept along as the Beast fought his way back to the shore. The distance between them grew.

He's abandoning us! That's great! First he gets us into this mess, then he abandons us! Stella freaked out.

Gillian saw the Beast reach the shallows and stand up. Stella was right. He was gone and she was totally alone. She cried out for help, then inhaled water as she was pulled under by a swirl in the current. She came up coughing and barely missed a large boulder.

She thought of the rocks looming ahead and spun around forward. She remembered hearing that if you were in a river, you needed to float on your back with your feet in front of you. That way, if you hit a rock, you would only break your leg, not your skull. Neither sounded very good, but she stuck her feet out in front of her anyway and kept them pointing downstream. She knew enough not to fight the current. Even if she was Michael Phelps, she wouldn't be able to swim against the rushing water. She would have to wait for a calm section so she could get to shore. Trying before that would only tire her out. Then she looked to the sides and realized there was no shore to get to. The riverbanks here were sheer cliffs. Even if she could swim across the current to get to the edge, there was nowhere to exit the river.

Gillian watched the canyon walls rush past and wondered how she would make her way back to camp. Then she heard a sound that made her heart try to jump right out of her chest and run away! The sound of water flowing had transformed into the sound of water falling. She gasped, recalling the Hunter story. There was a waterfall not too far from camp. A boy had almost gone over and the horse who saved him had gone over and died! She flailed her arms and kicked, trying to paddle backwards without coming out of her safety position. Her frantic movements had no effect. She felt a burst of pain as her right shoulder slammed into a rock, then another as her left hip hit one too. She saw another rock up ahead and tried to grab hold of it, but she was moving too quickly and the rock was too slippery. Luckily, the current was carrying her forward and the collisions were mostly side-swipes. But she felt like a pinball bouncing around, and she briefly pictured the rocks lighting up as she crashed into one after another.

She wasn't able to see it coming, but the sound grew louder. Suddenly she was moving faster, being sucked toward the edge of the waterfall. She was thrust out into the air, suspended for a moment, and then she was falling, and the river fell with her. The fall lasted for two seconds. She knew it was only two seconds; it didn't feel any longer than that, but as she fell, the tiniest details of each instant were burned into her brain. Every thought she had, everything she saw, some part of her knew she would be able to replay over and over like a movie in her head—if she survived the landing. Then she was several feet under white frothing water, being tumbled like clothes in a washing machine. She opened her eyes as wide as they would go, frantically looking up at the surface, but the force of the waterfall pinned her down. She realized she must have screamed as she fell because her lungs were empty. Just a few feet above her was the air she needed so badly, but she couldn't get to it.

She spun, trying to find a way out. Right beside her was a jagged boulder that would have sliced her open or broken several bones if she'd landed on it. The urge to breathe in was overwhelming but she forced her chest to clamp down tight, knowing that sucking water into her lungs could kill her. She braced her feet on the rock and shoved upward. But her boot slipped and got wedged into a crack in the boulder. She shook it, but it wouldn't come loose. She tried to kick off her boot but her foot wouldn't come out. She saw black spots in front of her eyes. Flailing and kicking hard, she looked up again to see how far she was from the surface, knowing her aching lungs couldn't hold on much longer. Then she saw in front of her the dark form of legs and a flowing tail.

Hunter! Stella whispered through the panic. Gillian thought the lack of oxygen must be making her hallucinate the ghost horse, but she reached out and grasped the tail as hard as she could. She hung on as the powerful legs kicked and her foot was wrenched free. The breath that was finally beyond her control started an instant before she broke the water's surface. Drops of water were pulled in with the breath and threw her into fits of coughing and retching, but somehow she kept hold of the ghostly tail. As she coughed and noisily gulped in air, she saw sparking lights. And then the bright afternoon sun flickered and went black as if someone had blown it out.

CHAPTER 13

GILLIAN AWOKE ON the bank of the river near the base of the waterfall. She was breathing clean cool air. She was breathing! It was the best feeling she had ever had! She pulled sweet, pine-scented air deep into her lungs, stretching out the sore muscles in her chest. The deep blue cloudless sky above her was stunning. She lay still for a few moments, amazed by its beauty. And by the fact that she was alive to see it. But she knew she had to get up if she could. She scanned herself for injuries. Her shoulder and hip ached where they had hit rocks, but all the joints and muscles seemed to move and flex the way she wanted them to. She carefully rolled her head to the side and realized she was still wearing her riding helmet. Sitting up, she pulled it off and was horrified by the spiderweb crack on its upper left side. Touching her head in that spot and rotating her neck in all directions, she was shocked there was no injury. Not even a bump.

She stood shakily and looked around. The opposite riverbank was a massive canyon wall that rose straight up out of the water. On her own side, the cliff face had ended at the waterfall. She stood on a low rocky shore that followed the river downstream as far as she could see.

She turned her back to the river. The shore sloped gradually upward away from water's edge. She walked a few metres up the slope, and the rocky ground gave way to dirt. Here there were a few scattered trees and then a wall of dense evergreen forest. In the distance she could see the hills rising up above the trees. She hobbled her way to the edge of the woods. There were no signs of civilization or of a trail of any kind, though on the softer ground she noticed some hoofprints leading into the trees.

Hunter! Stella whispered again.

"Will you stop saying that?" Gillian blurted. She knew she needed to do something, to get out of here, but her mind was whirling with images. The surface of the water far above her. Her foot caught in the boulder. The shadow of a ghost horse that had saved her life.

Stella's voice was sharp this time, bringing Gillian back to the present. *Well, this sucks. I mean, it's great that we survived and all that, but it's not like we can climb back up the waterfall. How exactly are you planning to get us out of this mess?*

Gillian was shaking badly. The heat of the day was beginning to wane. A breeze picked up, and her clothes were still soaking. Her teeth chattered and she realized she was standing in the shade. She moved to a sunny patch and jumped up and down to try to warm up.

Great! Jumping. That's fun. I don't see how it's going to get us rescued, but you're in charge. Stella was even more sarcastic than usual.

"Just let me think for a minute!" Gillian shouted.

Stella waited.

"Okay, well, I can't go back the way I came."

Nope, Stella agreed.

"I should stay put until someone rescues me. That's what you're supposed to do when you get lost."

If someone's even coming, said Stella.

Gillian continued, fighting hard against Stella's negativity. "The problem is it's getting cold. I have no idea how long it will take them to find me. For all they know I could be right here, or way downstream. And it's not like they can just hike down the waterfall."

You're assuming they think there's a chance we're still alive, said Stella.

Gillian felt dizzy. She sat down, hugging her knees. Her throat was sticky. She looked longingly at the river, wishing for a drink, but didn't want to chance getting sick from dirty water. She had no food or shelter either. She began again. "I could follow the ghost horse hoofprints into the woods."

Stella was quick to reply. *Do I really have to remind you how we feel about ghosts? Friendly or otherwise? Not too thrilled about getting lost in those woods either.*

"Yeah, okay, lost in the woods with a ghost sounds bad. Wait! If I walk along the riverbank downstream I should eventually meet the highway."

Yes! Highways are good. People. Civilization. No ghost horses. No scary woods. Stella was adamant.

"But I have no idea how far it is before the river meets up with the highway. The bus left the riverside a while before we got to camp," Gillian countered, aware that she was having an out-loud debate with her inner voice. Somehow, right then, it didn't seem that strange. Maybe she had hit her head harder than she realized.

Stella sighed. *Yup, we're totally going to die out here.*

Gillian sighed. "All the options suck, but downstream gives us a chance. Maybe we'll find a trail or some shelter or something." She stretched her slowly tightening muscles and began to walk along the rocky riverbank, leaving no footprints behind her.

LIBBY DIDN'T SCARE easily, but she had to fight to control the shaking she felt inside as she hung up the phone. She wasted no time, though. She grabbed her pack and flew down the steps of her cottage. Carmen caught up with her and they ran up the path to the stables together.

"I wish I could come with you and Robin," Carmen said.

"I need you here," said Libby. "We can't both be gone. We'll stay in radio contact as much as we can. Park rangers are on their way to help with the search but they won't be here for a few hours. They likely won't make it past the waterfall before dark."

"What about the helicopter?" Carmen asked.

"The storm has already hit Vancouver. The winds are too high for takeoff. If it settles down, they'll fly up first thing in the morning."

"Morning!" Carmen gasped.

Libby knew her head counsellor was picturing the young camper alone in the woods through the night. "That's why I need to get to her before dark."

"And her parents?" asked Carmen.

Libby winced at the question. She had felt physically ill when she made the phone call a few minutes ago. "Gillian's sister is at a training camp in Victoria. They made a weekend getaway out of it, and now ferries and flights have all been cancelled due to the winds. They can't get off the island. They asked me to please find Gillian and bring her back."

They arrived at the paddock and Libby turned to face Carmen. "I promised them you would contact them regularly with updates. I won't have cell service." She said this with no apology, even knowing how hard it would be for the young woman to speak to Gillian's frightened parents, and maybe have to deliver bad news.

Libby watched Carmen's initial horrified expression shift to a set jaw and a determined nod. "No problem," Carmen said.

Libby nodded and knew she was leaving the right person in charge.

JAIDA WAS AWARE she was riding up the trail back from the river. But she didn't remember how she got there. She remembered the water fight, and riding her horse into the river and laughing as they splashed through the water. She remembered screaming as Gillian floated away, and begging Naomi to go after her. She remembered lots and lots of tears. But she didn't remember leaving the clearing. The tears had stopped at some point. She didn't know why. She still felt awful. She couldn't even name what she felt. She had been sad and scared and angry in the past. This was worse than all of those. She glanced around. A few of the other girls were crying. Even Naomi was visibly shaken but, true to form, was trying to stay positive, reminding the girls that Libby was already on her way and if anyone could get Gillian back, it would be her. At a wider section near the top of the trail, Katrina rode up beside Jaida and said softly, "She's going to be okay."

Jaida turned and glared. "What are you talking about? How can you say that?"

Katrina looked down. "Because she has to be. I have to apologize."

"You mean because this is *totally your fault*?" said Jaida. "She never would have been on that *stupid* horse if it wasn't for *you*... She was headed for the waterfall. She could be..." Jaida couldn't finish the sentence.

Katrina squeezed her eyes shut, tears poking out at the corners.

Jaida's rage disappeared. She softened her tone. "There's nothing we can do and wishing it was different isn't going to bring her back."

"I know," said Katrina. Her voice wavered. "It's my fault. I didn't want this to happen but I caused it. That part's true. But there is something we can do. I have an idea."

THE CREATURE BREATHED raggedly as it pushed its way through the trees. It moved cautiously, peering out at the girl scrambling over the rocks by the river's edge. It stopped when she stopped. It watched her as she sat to pull off her boot and dump out the gravel that had built up inside. The girl had no idea the creature was there. The sounds of the river and the distance between them kept her from hearing its movements. It followed her, watching her slow, painful movements, noticing her hunger, her weakness and her despair. As she pushed on, it crept along with her, keeping itself hidden. It wanted to get closer, but instinct kept it sheltered in the trees. The creature could be patient. Soon, it knew, they would meet.

CHAPTER 14

GILLIAN DIDN'T HAVE a watch but it felt like hours had passed. She found it harder to make her legs keep taking steps. The temperature had dropped further and the wind had picked up. The sun had crawled past the edge of the cliff, leaving the entire riverbank in the shade. She thought it would be light out for a few more hours, which was good since her progress was achingly slow. Her riding boots weren't designed for scrambling over boulders and loose piles of rock. In some areas the bank narrowed to a thin ledge and in a few places she had to wade through small creeks that wound their way down from the woods. Her clothes still weren't dry and she was shivering even though she kept moving. Her muscles and joints were stiff and sore from her body being tossed around in the river. Her throat stuck to itself when she tried to swallow the tiny amounts of spit she was able to form. It was probably only just past dinnertime, but she felt like she was starving because she knew she had no way to get a meal or even a snack. She wanted nothing more than to sit down and wait to be rescued, but for all she knew, Stella was right and everyone had written her off for dead. She would have to get out of this on her own. For the first little while, she had forced herself to keep from crying to conserve body fluids. But as she stumbled and landed hard for the millionth time, the tears flowed freely. And then one more time Stella chimed in. *I bet you're pretty sorry you didn't listen to me when I said we should pretend to be sick. I mean, I hate to say I told you so, but...*

Gillian cut Stella off mid-sentence. "I didn't listen to you? All I ever do is listen to you! You never shut up! And you don't hate to say you told me so. It's your favourite thing to say! You never say anything positive, and I'm done! Shut up! Get out of my head and leave me alone!"

The words she yelled echoed in her ears louder than before. Stella was gone. Gillian was still on her hands and knees, breathing heavily, but she wasn't crying anymore. She sniffed a few times and stood, not really sure how to feel.

On some level, she knew Stella was not a real companion. She was a part of Gillian's own self that was more negative and self-conscious than what she allowed other people to see. Stella didn't make her feel less alone. But as Gillian searched her surroundings for signs of civilization, and became aware that she was totally on her own, she almost broke down and begged the voice to come back.

"No!" She clenched her fists, urging herself onward. "I can do this. This river meets the highway somewhere. I just have to keep going." She thought about the approaching nightfall and moved forward with new determination. She needed to get as far as she could with whatever sunlight she had left. She climbed over a large boulder and scrambled up another large mound of scree. She almost skied down the other side in a miniature rock avalanche, allowing herself a brief moment of fun. Then as she reached the bottom and the rocks stopped sliding under her feet, she heard rustling in the woods nearby. *Someone's in there*, she thought, rushing toward the sound with new-found energy. She reached the edge of the forest and took a tentative step in beyond the tree line.

“Hello? I’m lost. I’m just a kid and I need help. Please! Who’s there?” Gillian walked a few steps farther. The rustling got louder. She yelped as something bulky came bursting out from the underbrush. She gasped when she saw that it was the most adorable baby bear. He ran up to her and stood on his back legs. He didn’t even reach her shoulder. The furry creature dropped down onto all fours and bounded around her playfully, looking at her, trying to get her to join in. She spun around, watching him, at first amazed, and then suddenly terrified.

“Where’s your mama?” she whispered, trying to shoo him away. He stopped bounding and stared at her for a moment as if trying to figure out what she had said. She reached for the whistle on her wrist to try to scare him away, but it wasn’t there. She must have lost it in the river. Then came a deep growl from off to her right. She turned and saw the massive mama bear standing on two legs, fangs bared.

Gillian whimpered. She backed up slowly with her hands up as if the bear were holding a gun. “I’m sorry,” she pleaded. “I didn’t hurt him, I swear. Please. I’ll just go..." She bumped into a tree trunk. The bear opened its jaws and roared, walking forward a few steps. Gillian was frozen against the tree, eyes wide, heart pounding. She couldn't believe that after everything she'd managed to survive already, now she was about to be torn apart by a bear! She knew she could never outrun it. With black bears she knew she was supposed to try to scare them away, but having come between mama and baby, she seriously doubted that would work this time. And besides that, she couldn't find the strength to yell.

"Please..." she managed to squeak out again as she slid down the tree trunk and curled into a ball. As the bear dropped to all fours and lunged forward, she found her voice in time for one last scream. "No, no, *noooooooooo*!"

Hoofbeats pounded through the woods and a high-pitched whinny pierced the air. Mane and tail streaming behind, hooves flailing wildly, the General burst through the trees and charged the bear. He reared up and kicked the mama bear hard in the face with his forefoot. She shrieked with pain and confusion. The Beast continued to dance around her, legs flying out, landing kicks on the hulking animal, who had no idea what had hit her. The baby bear, frightened, ran to safety behind his mom and bleated. The mama bear screeched and then saw that her baby was out of danger. She decided she didn't want this fight. She spun and herded the cub away through the brush. The Beast gave a half-hearted cantering chase for a few moments, then turned and trotted back to Gillian, who was still crouched on the ground, too stunned to move. He stood over her, head lowered, snuffling her shoulder until she stopped shaking and stood up. They stared at each other for several seconds before she threw her arms around him and buried her face in his neck.

USUALLY WHEN LIBBY rode the trails at Canyon Falls she felt more at peace than she did anywhere else. This time, the wilderness felt cold and strange. She saw danger behind every tree. She heard it in every snapping twig and in the rushing sound of the river. She had chosen Robin to come with her for many reasons. Robin was Gillian's counsellor and Libby wanted someone the girl knew well to be there when they found her. Also, Robin had been born and raised in Lytton, so she knew the terrain well. Libby had ridden the trails countless times but it would be helpful to have someone who could help navigate. And they could split up if they had to, though that would only happen if absolutely necessary.

There was no possible way for Gillian to have escaped the river before heading over the falls. The same was true for the General. The counsellors had told Libby that he had been free of the current, but he had heard Gillian's cry for help and he turned back to go after her. So Libby and Robin were headed to the base of the waterfall. To get there they had to ride to the area where the girls had played in the water earlier in the day. Then they had to take a trail on the far side of the clearing. It wound through crevasses in the cliff and the terrain was steep and dangerous. Libby never allowed trail rides here for that reason. She knew that she and Robin had to travel safely but their pace was maddeningly slow. It was close to seven o'clock before they reached the lower bank and Libby felt sick not seeing Gillian waiting for them at the water's edge.

Libby and Robin separated and scoured the area. When she heard Robin yell that she had found both hoofprints and footprints in the mud by the edge of the tree line, Libby ran over, shaking with relief. The horse and the girl had both survived the waterfall and were well enough to be up and walking around! The hoofprints led into the woods, but the footprints were scattered and hard to follow. They went in a few circles, seemed to stop in different places and it was impossible to tell where they finished as the soft ground turned to rock closer to the riverbank. Because the hoofprints leading away from the river kept going and the footprints disappeared, Libby and Robin decided that Gillian must have eventually mounted the horse and they had gone off into the woods together. Maybe she thought she could find a trail back up above the waterfall. They had figured she might try to meet the highway farther down the river, but that wasn't where the prints led. They could only try to guess what Gillian had been thinking.

While relieved at having found evidence of the pair still alive, Libby knew they had to work quickly. With the cold front coming through, strong wind, rain, hail and no gear, Gillian would be at high risk of hypothermia. She could be injured. And then there was the wildlife... bears, cougars, wolf packs, coyotes...

Knowing their time was limited, the search party of two followed the hoofprints into the trees, moving as quickly as the dense forest would allow. There was no way they could have known the prints would lead them deep into the woods and disappear.

CHAPTER 15

GILLIAN AND THE Beast walked together back to the riverbank. She rambled to him, just happy to have someone to talk to. "I must have been pretty low on oxygen back there to think I was rescued by a ghost horse. Of course it was you. Probably just trying to make up for getting us into this mess in the first place. Thanks, though. I guess that's twice now that you've saved my life. Pretty wild ride over the falls, eh?" Gillian turned to continue her trek downstream, but the Beast stopped at the water's edge and refused to move. She turned to look at him. "Are we going to be fighting again already? The highway is this way. We need to keep moving."

He neighed and tossed his head. He turned upstream, walked a few steps and then turned back to look at her. She stood staring at him with her arms crossed. He turned away and walked farther upstream, stopping again to look back after a few moments.

Gillian shrugged and said, "Fine! We'll do it your way. I have no idea what I'm doing out here anyway. Maybe you do. If the ground wasn't so rocky I'd get back in the saddle and..." Her words trailed off as she realized he was still wearing the saddle. She ran to his right side, reached into the front saddlebag and pulled out her water bottle. "Yes!" she cheered. Finally something had gone her way. She gulped half of what was left before forcing herself to stop. She had no idea how long this would have to last her. She sealed the bottle and put it back into the pouch, feeling a little stronger. "Okay, let's go," she said.

The two of them scrambled over the rocks Gillian had worked so hard to get past in the other direction not long before. But they hadn't gone more than a few hundred metres when the horse stopped again and refused to keep going. He stared out across the river.

"Now what?" she demanded. "What is wrong with you? You're the one who wanted to go this way in the first place! Why am I following you? You're just a dumb..." Her words trailed off again. She followed his gaze out across the river. About halfway across, a fallen tree stuck out from the water. Caught on a branch were a soccer ball and a large bright yellow balloon. On the side of the balloon, if she squinted just right, she could see her own name written in giant bubble letters.

The Beast snorted and gave Gillian a nudge toward the river.

She turned to gape at him. "That's it! I've totally lost my mind. I'm hallucinating. You're probably not even here. I was killed by that bear back there. I'm dead. I'm dead and this isn't real... and... wait, that's not a balloon." She had just noticed the black strap dangling off the end. "It's a pack! It's a dry bag! With my name on it. Beast, what's going on?" The horse nudged her again toward the water.

She turned and glared at him. "You go get it! You're the one who likes to swim so much!" He simply stared at her. She shook her head, sighed and sat down heavily on the bank as the realization set in. "Right. No hands to unhook it from the branch." She was going to have to go back into the river. She sat for a few minutes, trying to figure out how she was going to get the bag. She didn't want to risk getting swept away again. Then she stood up and looked at the animal.

"Okay," Gillian said, "but you're going to have to give me a hand. Hoof. You know what I mean."

The current was fairly strong, so she and the Beast walked upstream from where the bag was caught. This way the current would help move her downstream diagonally toward the bag. When she thought they had walked far enough upstream, she stopped and undressed down to her swimsuit. Then she untied the long lead line that had been hooked over the Beast's saddle and tied it around her waist. The other end was still hooked to his bridle. She stood for a moment, bracing herself against the thought of the cold water when she was already freezing. The Beast pawed at the ground and snorted impatiently.

"Hold your horses!" she said to him. He stared at her and she could have sworn he raised an eyebrow. It was the same look she gave her dad when he told a dumb joke. Gillian burst out laughing. "Yep, definitely losing my mind a little. Telling bad jokes to a horse." She sighed and waded into the water. It felt even colder than it had that afternoon. Was that really only a few short hours ago? She shook her head with disbelief and began to swim. She had been right about working with the current. She was travelling on a diagonal and quickly approached the log. However, she was still a good metre and a half away from it when she felt the tug of the rope around her waist. She couldn't swim any farther.

She turned to look back at the Beast standing on the bank. "Come forward, Beast!" she yelled. She eggbeater-kicked to keep herself in place in the current and ran her hands over the lead rope toward herself. The Beast tossed his head and stepped into the river toward her. When she had enough give in the rope, she waved her finger at him and he stopped instantly. She swam a few more short strokes and reached the log. She was able to free the strap quickly and slung it over her shoulder.

She swam back toward the shore. She aimed downstream so she was swimming with the current, which should have made it easier, but her fingers and toes were numb. Her arms were stiff and her legs were heavy. Her usually powerful stroke was now weak and ineffective. Her breaths were short and gasping. Her thoughts flashed back to being pinned deep under the surface. Then she heard the Beast whinny. He stared out at her, moving nervously back and forth in the shallow water. She grabbed the rope attached to her waist and lifted it out of the water, shaking it from side to side. Instantly, the anxious animal backed out of the water onto the riverbank. His movement pulled her closer to the shore. She shook the rope more. He kept backing up until she was able to stand in the shallow water. She signalled for him to stand still and she used the rope to pull herself up the bank. As soon as she was out, he trotted over to her and stood close.

She grabbed her shirt off the saddle and pulled it over her head. She regretted that it was still wet, but she needed to warm up. Then she sat down with the bag. It was a large dry sack that had the weight of a fair bit of gear, along with some air to keep it afloat. It looked like the soccer ball was added afterwards for extra flotation. She untied it from the bag and held it up in her hand. The Beast stood over her and nosed the ball from her grasp. He kicked it lightly and went after it, but didn't stray too far from Gillian. She watched him for a minute, amazed.

"You recognized the ball," she said, marvelling. "You brought me here so I would swim out and get your toy." He looked at her, then dropped his nose to the ground and pushed the ball toward Gillian. She laughed and rolled it back to him. He stopped it with a hoof and then wandered a few steps away to munch at a patch of grass.

Gillian unclipped the rolled top of the dry bag and opened it. The first thing she pulled out was a large lightweight towel, which she immediately wrapped around her shivering body. The next items she found were a water-filtration pump, a full water bottle and a zipper-lock plastic bag full of granola bars, bags of trail mix and dried fruit. She ripped open two of the granola bars and inhaled them before exploring the rest of the bag. There were two full sets of dry clothes, a fleece jacket, a hat, gloves, a headlamp, a lightweight sleeping bag, a ground sheet and a few small tarps, several lengths of rope, matches, a fire-starter candle, some newspaper, a first aid kit, Fluffy and another zipper-lock plastic bag with paper inside. Fluffy? What on earth was going on?

Gillian quickly dried herself with the towel, changed out of her wet swimsuit into dry clothes, ate some trail mix and drank almost the entire bottle of water. She figured out how to use the pump and refilled the bottle for later. Finally feeling full and warmish for the first time in hours, she opened the bag with the paper inside, and found it was a letter.

Dear Gillian,

We're sending this bag of supplies floating down the river hoping that it finds you. If you're reading this then you've survived some unbelievable stuff today and we're all out there in the woods with you right now. Not really, but you know what I mean.

Try not to be afraid. We passed Libby and Robin on the trail back to camp. They brought extra gear in case it takes them a while to find you. They won't give up. Search and Rescue is coming too but Libby and Robin have a head start. We told them about our plan to send this pack and Libby said to tell you to try to stay along the riverbank and not to go too far downstream. It would take you days to get to the highway. Robin said to hang in there. They'll be there as soon as they can.

We hope we've sent you everything you need to keep you warm and fed for as long as it will take. Help is on the way.

Oh, and by the way, this was all Katrina's idea. Thought you should know that. She feels horrible about the whole situation. I said she should write something here too, but she said she has to apologize in person when you get back.

We love you and miss you, Gillian. Come back. Please!

And bring Fluffy with you if you can.

Jaida and everyone else.

Gillian was stunned. Suddenly she felt about ten degrees warmer. Some of her strength returned along with the food and hope of rescue. She packed up her new gear and walked with the Beast a little ways downstream until they came to a place where they could camp. She tied the horse's long lead rope to a tree by a clearing and removed his saddle, laying it across a fallen log. He sighed gratefully and moved off to graze, but not too far away. She sat beside the saddle. She was exhausted and almost cried again at the thought of having to set up a shelter, gather wood and light a fire before she could rest. She was grateful for the supplies that her friends had sent, but she'd never done anything like this before. Sure, she'd been camping, but her dad had always set up the tent and tarps while her mom got the fire going. She and Alexis usually went off exploring while that stuff was going on. She slid off the log onto the ground and hugged her knees. She dropped her face onto her arms and cried. Big loud gulping shaking cries. Her nose ran. Her eyes swelled. Her chest ached. The Beast stood over her the entire time, ears pricked toward the forest, listening for any threat. But eventually she could breathe again and she lifted her head. She shakily got to her feet and opened the bag of gear. She could do this. She didn't really have much choice.

She had picked this spot by the river to camp because of the trees. The dense forest was still several metres away but there were some scattered tall pines right down to the river's edge. They were sparse enough that she could light a fire, but close enough together that she could tie the tarps to them for shelter. She folded one tarp around a tree to make a corner, so she had two walls to block the wind. Then she strung the other tarp up to form a slanted roof to keep off the rain if it came. She used some of the knots they had learned for tying up the horses. She hoped they would hold. She gathered a thick layer of pine needles so sleeping would be a little more cushioned and she would be insulated from the cold ground. She found some brush and some larger sticks and logs from the edge of the woods, reluctant to venture too far in after her earlier experience with the bear. Her fire pit was a circle of stones she had made under her roof, but near the edge so she wouldn't get smoked out. With the walls of her shelter blocking the increasing wind, she was able to get a small fire going and she warmed up a bit more. As dusk crept in, her camp was finally set up. She looked it over. It wasn't perfect or even pretty, but she had to admit it was pretty good.

She took off the Beast's lead rope. She wanted him to be able to get to the river to drink, and to graze and to get to the shelter if he needed to. She didn't think he would leave her again. She tied his soccer ball to a nearby tree so he could kick it around the camp if he wanted to. She gave him a long scratch around the ears and he sighed.

"Maybe I should try listening to you more often," she told him. "Maybe I could have avoided this whole mess myself. You must have been so hot after that trail ride. And then you had to stand there on the shore watching us all play in the water. You wanted to get in too, didn't you? You just wanted to play and cool off." He nuzzled her neck before giving the ball a few good kicks, and then he walked slowly off to go get himself some dinner.

Gillian sat down on a rock by the fire with a bag of trail mix.

Wow. Look what you did, said the familiar voice.

"Stella!" Gillian almost fell off the rock with surprise. "Where did you go?" she asked.

Umm, you sent me away. Remember?

"You've never gone away when I told you to before."

This was the first time you meant it.

"Sorry. I..."

Gillian, remember who you're talking to here. You've always doubted yourself. But this time it could've killed you. You needed to send me away and you did. Pretty sweet campsite!

"I'm not saved yet," Gillian said.

True. Somebody else still needs to come to the rescue. But you've done everything you can until they do. I'm kind of... proud of you. Hey, you get what that means, don't you? Stella asked and then faded into Gillian's thoughts, because Gillian did get what it meant. Despite being alone, frightened and unsure of what the night or the following day would bring, she was intensely proud of herself.

CHAPTER 16

ROBIN FOUGHT TO keep the stove lit in the wind while she tried to cook a quick dinner. She saw that Libby was having a similar battle with the tent. The soup finally started to simmer in the pot. Robin had no appetite but she would eat, because she would need to be strong tomorrow. She and Libby had followed the hoofprints into the trees for about an hour, but the underbrush was so thick that they lost the trail. They scoured the surrounding forest with no luck. Several precious hours of searching and calling left them with sore throats and tired horses. They made their way back to the river a short distance downstream from where they had started. With the darkness and the wind, they knew they had to stop searching for the night and set up camp.

As they sat and ate, Robin tried to think of things

to say. She was desperate to distract herself from the horrible thoughts in her head. But nothing seemed appropriate. At one point she tried, "Wow, that wind is really howling." But Libby just stared at her. Neither of them could think of anything besides their lost camper and what she might be going through. So, mostly in silence, they finished supper, tidied up and got ready for sleep. They had tried several times to make contact with Carmen to let her know they had found evidence that Gillian and the General were alive, but they couldn't get a signal. The oncoming storm must have been interfering. Robin wasn't thrilled to be camping in the wilderness in a storm with no contact, but that wasn't her biggest concern. Not tonight. She lay in the dark, eyes wide open, unable to settle. For what seemed like hours, images of bears and cougars ran through her mind. The wind was ferocious. She was so frightened for Gillian. She was physically exhausted but her mind wouldn't stop. She couldn't just lie there, but didn't know what else to do. She rolled to one side, then flipped to the other. Then the rain started. Lightly at first and then battering the tent. Robin sat up suddenly, running her hands through her hair.

Libby lay facing away from Robin. She didn't move, but finally she spoke. "We're not going back without her." Her voice was calm and determined, with no hint of sleep in it.

"Libby," Robin began.

"I messed up," Libby went on. "She should never have been on that horse. These girls and their parents trust me. I didn't live up to that trust. Not finding her is not an option."

"Libby, you didn't..."

"There's no way to look at it so that it's not my fault. I am fully responsible. Which is why we need to get some sleep. We need to be fresh and thinking clearly as soon as it's light out."

Robin stared at Libby's back, amazed at how practical and calm she was on the outside. She lay back down, doing her best to follow her boss's example.

Eventually she slept, but she dreamed of a young girl shivering and alone on a riverbank in the storm.

GILLIAN WAS STARTLED awake by a frantic whinny as the Beast charged out of the shelter. She called after him but he didn't come back. She was too cold and frightened to follow him out into the night. It was pitch-dark. The clouds blocked out any moonlight and the fire was out. She huddled deep in her sleeping bag, clutching Fluffy and shivering violently.

When it first got dark, she'd been relatively comfortable. The fire had still burned. The Beast had stood nearby, watching over her. She'd been feeling optimistic about early morning rescue. Exhaustion had taken over and she'd slept. Now it was deep into the night and the wind raged against her flimsy shelter. Her tarps shook loudly and strained against the knots she had tied. And she was alone. She lay hugging herself and the little white bunny, listening for sounds of what might be out there. Then the rain started. A few drops at first. Then more. Within minutes the sound of the rain pounding drowned out everything else. Her thin walls and roof rattled and jumped. The knots held even as the downpour picked up strength. But the air was damp and Gillian ached with cold. She turned on the headlamp to try to spot the Beast but the beam only lit up the driving storm. And so she squeezed her eyes shut, covered her ears with her hands and waited for a creature to come and tear her to pieces. Every second that passed was a second closer to morning and a second longer that she survived. She hung on to that thought as she shivered.

THE CABIN SEEMED darker than usual to Katrina. She had no idea what time it was, but it was late. Exhausted but unable to sleep, she stared across the room at Gillian's bunk. She could just make out the flat, empty sleeping bag, and the little stuffed pony lying on the pillow. Jaida sniffled softly in her own bed. Emiko and Mira whispered on the bunks above. For once, Naomi didn't shush them. Only Jordan lay silent and still. Katrina wasn't able to see her face but she was sure the older girl lay staring at the bed above her, wishing it would creak with the movements of her friend. It wouldn't. Not tonight.

The wind shrieked and shook the cabin, as if it was trying to get inside. *It's angry at me*, Katrina thought, *just like everyone else*. She rolled to face the wall and put the pillow over her head but it didn't block out the sound. She felt numb. She hugged her arms around herself, trying to feel something else. She'd been angry earlier, when she'd been dumped here by her mom, when Jordan had told her off, when Gillian had been so perfect all the time. Then when Jordan got hurt, the anger had twisted to shame and guilt. But now, when it was Katrina's fault that her cabin mate was missing and in danger, all she could feel was a dull aching emptiness.

The rain started. A few drops at first, but soon it was pounding loudly on the roof. Katrina watched Jaida as she squirmed fitfully and whimpered. Her gaze then flicked back to Gillian's bed, her pillow, the pony. Suddenly Katrina sat bolt upright, narrowly missing smashing her head on the bottom of Mira's bunk. Then she was out of bed and across the cabin. She stepped up on Jordan's bed frame and reached up.

"Katrina, what are you doing?" asked Jordan, shocked.

Katrina climbed back down and walked over to Jaida, who stared up at her with wide, tearful eyes.

"Elfkin is worried," Katrina said to Jaida as she held out the pony. "She could probably use a hug."

Jaida took the stuffy and squeezed her tightly.

Katrina climbed back into bed. She realized that numb and helpless felt an awful lot the same. She didn't like either one. She still couldn't sleep.

CHAPTER 17

GILLIAN OPENED HER eyes and was instantly confused. All she knew was that wherever she was, it was warm. Home in her room, maybe... No, that wasn't right. The cabin at camp... But there had been no bell and the mattress didn't feel right. Plus she was nestled up against someone, which was weird. She hadn't even shared a bed with her sister in years. Also, she was wrapped in some sort of slippery fabric with a zipper. She wriggled around until she was able to pop her head out of the sleeping bag. And then she remembered.

Gillian was amazed that the walls of her shelter still stood. She looked over her shoulder and found herself pressed up against the Beast's wide back. The big horse must have lain down next to her after he returned in the middle of the night when she couldn't stop shivering. He was lying with his head raised, looking over his shoulder, watching her. When he saw that she was awake, he rolled away from her, stood up and shook himself gently. Then he walked down to the riverbank to graze.

Gillian realized she was roasting. She squirmed her way out of the sleeping bag and peeled off three layers of clothes. The storm had passed, the wind had died down and the night had rolled over into day. She stretched and twisted, trying to work out the stiffness. Walking out of the shelter, she noticed a few broken branches on the ground, but her knots had held and her supplies were all still there. She had survived the night. But the sun was creeping higher into the sky and no one had come for her yet. Where were they? Was something wrong? Why was it taking so long?

She then noticed how far the Beast's hoofprints were scattered around the campsite. She wasn't surprised that he'd been grazing in the grassy areas, but what had he been doing out behind the shelter, where there were only pine needles, mud and rocks? She walked slowly over to that area, studying the ground as she went. She inhaled sharply as she came across an enormous cat paw print in the mud, then several more. A cougar had stalked her camp last night. The General must have fought it off when he went running out of the tent during the storm. Shocked, she looked at the horse calmly grazing on the riverbank. She walked over to him and he lifted his head, leaning into her for a scratch.

"Thank you," she whispered into his twitching ear. She had never loved an animal more.

Gillian heard a loud snap in the trees. The Beast pulled away from her and took off galloping toward the sound. *The cougar*, she thought. She stood frozen in place, staring after him. She whipped her head around, looking for a place to hide. Then out of the trees burst Robin on her horse, yelling, "Libby! Over here! She's here! She's here!"

Suddenly Gillian's legs unfroze and she ran to her counsellor, who gracefully leaped from her horse. The two girls met in a bone-crunching hug as Libby flew out of the trees and whooped with relief. Gillian sobbed nonsense words into Robin's shoulder while Robin laughed and hugged tighter.

A little while later, Gillian sat sipping hot chocolate from a thermos while Robin and Libby took down her campsite and packed up her gear. The rescuers marvelled at her use of the tarps and her ability to tie knots as they struggled to undo them. She kept them amazed with her stories of survival from the day before.

Once they were packed and ready to go, Libby tacked up the Beast and began to climb into his saddle.

"Libby, wait. That's not your horse." Gillian went to stand at his head. He rested his chin on her shoulder. She reached up and tugged gently on his mane.

Libby stopped, foot in stirrup, and looked at Gillian. "He's not a camp horse anymore," she said.

"He's my partner. I'm riding him home." Gillian said calmly.

Libby gaped at her. "No. He's not safe. He's unpredictable. You could have been—"

"Yes, I could have been killed lots of times," agreed Gillian. "The reason I'm still here is because of this horse. He saved me more times than I can count. I'm riding him home and for the rest of the summer. Not because you put us together, but because he's my partner."

Libby opened her mouth and closed it again. Gillian stood in the older woman's gaze, feeling a confidence and self-assuredness she had never felt before. The big paint horse nuzzled her arm.

Libby shook her head, astonished. She stepped back and Gillian climbed into the saddle. The Beast seemed to sigh with satisfaction. Libby climbed into her own saddle and they started for camp.

GILLIAN HEARD THE chatter as she, Libby and Robin rounded the last corner of the trail to Canyon Falls. The radio had finally worked so Libby had called ahead that they had found the lost pair and were on their way back. The whole camp had been waiting on the Range for over an hour. Most of them were holding "Welcome Home" signs.

The cheer that erupted as the trio of riders emerged from the trail was overwhelming. Tears flowed down Gillian's cheeks, this time of joy and relief. As she rode with her rescuers into the crowd, she was surrounded and helped by several hands to dismount. Jordan, cast and crutches and all, was the first one to grab her in a tight hug. "So good to see you, Fidget," she said.

Second was Jaida. When they parted, Gillian pulled Fluffy from her jacket and handed her to the sobbing girl. "What were you thinking sending her when you had no idea if I was even alive?"

Jaida smiled through her tears. "I knew you were alive. Katrina said you had to be. And I figured you needed Fluffy more than I did last night."

Gillian grinned at her friend and was then caught up in another hug, this time from Emiko, who for once couldn't find any words. Then it was Naomi, then Mira, then Carmen. She was passed from one set of arms to another. The celebration went on for several minutes before Libby finally grabbed Gillian by the arm and pulled her away from the crowd toward her cottage. The huge welcome was really nice but all Gillian actually wanted was a hot meal, a shower and to sleep for about a week. So she was happy to go with Libby. But before she did that, she searched the crowd and eventually found Katrina, who stood apart, off to the side, eyes downcast. Gillian pulled out of Libby's grip and approached her. Katrina opened her mouth to speak but before she could get the words out, Gillian wrapped her in a tight, heartfelt hug. "Thank you!" she said.

Katrina returned the hug for a moment, but then pushed away. "I'm so sorry. It was my fault you were out there—"

"Oh, get over yourself already," Gillian interrupted, rolling her eyes with mock annoyance, then grinning. Katrina looked shocked. "You made one mistake. I mean, don't get me wrong, it was a pretty bad mistake. But everything that happened after that just happened on its own. You don't control the whole universe." Her voice was sincere now as she continued. "All I know is I wouldn't have made it through last night without all that stuff. So thank you."

Katrina paused for a moment to absorb Gillian's words. She nodded and then said, "In that case, I'm glad I could help." And then Katrina smiled a huge smile, looking happy for the first time that Gillian had seen all summer.

EPILOGUE

Dear Lex,

It was really great to see you guys. I feel terrible that everyone had to be so worried about me. I wanted to say thanks for sticking up for me. I know mom and Dad think I'm crazy to stay here, and even crazier to keep working with the General. I know you probably do too. But since you're the one who convinced them to let me make the choice, I wanted you to understand it. I haven't lost my mind. I promise. I won't be playing in the river on the Beast again any time soon. But I really think that he and I have a lot to learn from each other. Basically the problem started because I wasn't paying attention to what he needed. Then he went a little crazy, and we got into a pretty bad situation. But he realized that he messed up and then he risked his life to save mine about sixty-four times. Since we've been back at camp, he's followed every command I've given him. And I'm doing my best to make sure I know what he needs as well.

So don't worry about me. I'm good. Actually, I'm great. I went over a waterfall, got attacked by a bear and spent a night out alone in the woods in a storm. And I survived! I needed a little help, but hey, who doesn't?

I'll be home really soon. I can't wait to watch you race in a few weeks. In fact, I can't wait to get back into the pool myself. Yes, I'm going to keep swimming. It's part of what saved me out there. But I'm going to keep riding too. And next summer, I'm coming back here.

Miss you tons and see you soon,

Love, Gilly

ACKNOWLEDGEMENTS

MY HUSBAND, JEFF, was my first reader. I think we were both equally nervous for him to read it and both equally relieved that he liked it. His support and enthusiasm mean the world to me... and so does he.

I knew my brother Rob, with his wealth of experience, his upfront honesty and his exceptionally thorough analysis, would be exactly what I needed with my first draft. His insights were invaluable. He has my greatest appreciation and admiration.

Immeasurable thanks also to Mom and Dad, my biggest and longest-running fans. They always knew I could do it, which allowed me to try.

Several of the characters were inspired by the deeply caring staff at Camp Ak-O-Mak in Ahmic Harbour, Ontario. These keen and enthusiastic women work intensely hard to ensure an incredible experience for the campers. It is an amazing place where girls are empowered and are encouraged to reach for the extraordinary. Canyon Falls is different in many ways, but I hoped to capture something of the Ak-O-Mak spirit.

I am also grateful to Heather Dow, who provided me with a deeper understanding of the psychology and intricacies of the natural horsemanship style of training and riding. Her insights were invaluable to the story.

And of course, thank you to the team at Harbour Publishing for taking a chance on this first-time author. Thanks especially to Brianna Cerkiewicz for the editorial feedback that made this story so much stronger.

ABOUT THE AUTHOR

SARI COOPER IS a doctor and writer. She was inspired to write *The Horse of the River* after a horseback riding and rafting trip in New Zealand (which included some harrowing experiences). She lives in Victoria, BC.